Jim Early's Law

When Jim Early rode into the ramshackle desert town of Zanzibar he had his long-legged fancy woman, a pocket full of money, and his freedom.

Twenty-four hours later and he has been robbed of $20,000 at a poker table, shot a man who tried to cheat him and inexplicably been appointed town marshal. But there's much more to come for Jim Early, and another hired gun is on his way to Zanzibar, looking to take the only thing Early has left: his life. Can matters get worse?

Jim Early's Law

Logan Winters

A Black Horse Western

ROBERT HALE · LONDON

ISBN 978-0-7198-1294-1

Robert Hale Limited
Clerkenwell House
Clerkenwell Green
London EC1R 0HT

www.halebooks.com

Typeset by
Derek Doyle & Associates, Shaw Heath
Printed and bound in Great Britain by
CPI Antony Rowe, Chippenham and Eastbourne

ONE

Poker can be a deadly game. Jim Travers was holding four queens in a game of seven-card stud and he wasn't about to fold to the two black aces Ben Lytle was showing on the table. All of his spare cash, some that wasn't spare, and some that wasn't even his, was on the table when the last card was dealt. Jim barely glanced at the three of diamonds he was dealt last. He didn't care which card filled his hand unless it was a fifth queen and that seemed unlikely, even with Ben Lytle dealing.

Ben called and uneasily threw in the last of the coin he was holding. Jim followed suit, smiled and waited. Lytle had nothing that could beat him. Jim had one of the red aces Ben had been looking for already dealt face-down to him. He smiled again, prematurely as it turned out. For Lytle had nothing in his hand that could beat four ladies, but in his other hand a .41-caliber derringer had appeared. Jim had nothing that could beat that.

'Well, Jim, it looks like I got you,' Lytle said, rising from the table.

'That happens sometimes when you sit down to a

card game, Ben. However, I never took you for such a low-down snake. I let you get by with your crooked dealing, but I didn't think you'd go to pulling iron on me.'

Jim decided to tip back in his chair and light one of the thin cigars David Austin had brought up from Mexico for him. There really wasn't much else to do at that point.

'I got debts, Jim; you don't understand.'

'Everyone has debts, Ben. A poker table is not one of the best places to try to catch up.'

'You just don't understand,' Ben said, shoveling coin and paper money into his traveling bag. Ben was sweating heavily under his arms, on his chest. He was a soft, round man with a bald head. There were beads of sweat on his pink forehead. He held the little derringer steady, though.

Jim had his Colt revolver riding on his hip, but there was no way he was going to bring it up and fire before Ben had drilled him with his purse-sized .41, so he didn't give that more than a second's thought. But he would have his money back from the card shark.

Ben wasn't the only one having money problems. Jim had his own trouble and it was every bit as important as Ben's was to him. For now, though, there was nothing to do but bide his time. A few men standing at the bar or sitting at other tables in the saloon were watching them, but the action wasn't even interesting enough to cause comment. Men with a pistol on the table were pretty much an everyday sight in the remote town of Zanzibar.

It was a good place for a man like Ben Lytle to drop anchor for a while. The town had no lawman, no honest citizens' brigade. It was run, and usually dominated, by the man with the first-drawn weapon. You might have called Zanzibar an outlaw town except there weren't enough really hard men for it to be considered as such.

Take for instance, Jim Early Travers. Jim was considered one of the town's most dangerous men. He even had paper out on him for bank robbery. Jim had never actually robbed that bank, had never even shot but three men – one of them accidentally – but in Zanzibar he was rated as a man to be wary of.

Jim had that reputation, which was helpful for getting along in a small frontier town. Which was the second reason that he couldn't let Ben Lytle get away with hijacking his coin; he had his image to protect. The first reason was . . . well, we'll come to her later.

'Thanks, Travers,' Ben said, for he had finished scooping the money into a green traveling bag with wooden handles that he had been carrying. 'No hard feelings?' he said, and it was a question. Jim smiled and shook his head, blowing a fairly regular smoke ring, which rose like a blue wreath toward the ceiling, slowly dissipating.

'No,' Jim said. 'Every game's a gamble, only the rules change. Hell, life's a gamble, isn't it, Ben? One minute you're bouncing along with a smile on your face, your bag filled with coin, the next you're lying dead on your face in the street.'

Ben Lytle didn't like that one. Jim saw his eyes flash,

7

and thought for a minute that he might pull the trigger on the derringer, but that was one thing that didn't go, even in this rough town. If a citizen of Zanzibar could just go around shooting people at random with no real cause, there was no telling who might be next. And Jim Early Travers remained one of the town's foremost citizens – for whatever that was worth.

Lytle stood, pushed his chair back, and sidestepped away from the table, his eyes trying to look in all directions at once. He might have thought that Jim had friends ready to jump into the dispute, with him having only two bullets in the derringer at his service. Lytle hadn't been around long enough to know that Jim had no friends – no one in Zanzibar had. They had drinking partners, men they nodded to on the street, a few they had bumped into in other places, but not friends.

Zanzibar was just a place you stayed to try to stay alive long enough to leave. Ben Lytle had missed the entire point of local etiquette. Any man in that saloon who knew Jim Travers, knew Zanzibar, knew that as soon as Ben Lytle passed through the door Jim would be on his feet and after him. He couldn't sit by and lose a poke that large and not have his own reputation ruined.

No sooner than Lytle had cleared the door, Jim was on his feet and in pursuit. His cigar lay smoldering on the floor and his hand was empty. He did not want to draw his Colt unless Lytle made a further issue of it. No one in the Red Bird Saloon would have found fault with him if he shot the little swindler, but there was always the messy problem of getting rid of the body to consider. Besides, Jim Early Travers was not a man who believed in killing.

The sun was bright in the street, glaring into his eyes. Jim had to pause for a moment and search for Lytle. Finally he saw him a few blocks away. The chubby man could scamper quicker than Jim had thought. Well, if a man thinks the Devil may be on his shirt-tail, he's likely to move more rapidly than usual.

Jim set off at a lope, not believing he would have to break into a dead run to catch the chubby man with much shorter legs. Besides, how long could Lytle keep up his current pace? The street was thronged with the usual knots of layabouts and the few honest business-men who worked along the street, loading and unloading merchandise. A heavy wagon carrying barrels of water rolled past, and Lytle used it to cover his dash to the far side of the street.

Lytle looked back at Jim, and Jim could see the panic on his pale face. He lifted his derringer as if he would fire, but did not. Jim continued to jog after the man. Lytle dashed through a group of three men, spinning one of them around. He was nearing the end of town now where the Strawberry Heights Hotel, the place Jim used as his residence in Zanzibar, stood on one corner, a feed and grain store on another, a small restaurant called Ethel M's on a third. Beyond this the town petered out. A few small-frame houses and three or four adobes were there, but the road soon met the skirts of the high desert country beyond.

Lytle had no place left to run. Watching Lytle as he bent over, huffing away, Jim saw with a jolting realiza-tion that Ben Lytle did not have the green traveling bag

9

with him. Where could he have secreted it? Jim continued to jog toward the round man. Lytle's face contorted, his eyes grew wider, and he again raised his derringer. This time he fired. Jim saw the puff of smoke from the small pistol's muzzle, felt a bullet whip past his head. That was it for Jim. If the gambler had only his derringer, as Jim believed, he had only one shot left. But each step was bringing Jim into closer range. Did he want to risk Lytle shooting again? No.

Jim halted and braced himself, drawing his big .44 Colt as he did so. Ben Lytle lifted his little pistol again, sighting down the barrel; Jim Early shot him dead.

Jim walked nearer, keeping his revolver in his hand. He let his eyes search the weed-ridden vacant lot, but could see nothing of the green bag containing the money. In front of the hotel across the street a small crowd had gathered, drawn by the sound of the shots. Behind Jim along the street a group of men approached, most of them from the Red Bird Saloon wanting to see how matters had played out.

Jim saw them all, did not see them. His attention was only on the green bag, or its absence. He approached Lytle's body to assure himself that his eyes had not been playing tricks on him, but there was no sign of the traveling bag behind or beneath the dead man. Lytle had either hidden it or passed it off, perhaps to someone among the group of men he had run through.

The only thing to do was to retrace their path. With luck some idea might occur to him as a possible hiding place. Of course if Lytle had hidden it carelessly it might have been recovered within moments, and Jim

Early had no illusions about the character of the local residents. No Zanzibar denizen was going to rush to Jim to return the stolen cash.

Angrily shoving his pistol back into its holster, he about-faced and started down the street again. He had to push past the small group of men there, taking no time to answer their questions. There was nothing he could tell them that they didn't already know.

The sun was hot on his back as he returned along the dusty street in the direction of the Red Bird. He caught himself grinding his teeth and forced himself to stop. From rich man to pauper in a matter of seconds! But at least no one in Zanzibar – well, one person excepted – was going to mourn Ben Lytle's loss. That was just the way things were on the fringe of civilization.

The situation caused Jim's thoughts to return to the one time in his life that he had done the right thing. The one time that he did not regret. But he had paid for it.

Down in Clovis, New Mexico Territory, Jim Early and two brothers named Hinton had decided that they were tired of eating lizard stew, and, being fine upstanding men, deserved better in life. They had made their way individually into the town's bank one morning and decided with glances to allow the elderly farm couple in front of them to finish their business before they found out what could be had from the bank's safe.

While Jim lounged indolently near the pair of sun-browned, time-wrinkled sodbusters, he overheard a part of their conversation.

'I can sleep nights now, Caleb,' the old woman in a

blue bonnet and sun-faded dress said to her older, taller husband. 'I thought we'd never bring the crop in this year. Then I was worried that Fred Sears wouldn't buy it.'

'Well, now we've got enough money for the seed crop next year,' the old man answered, nodding his head. His hands, Jim noticed, were time-worn and work-aged. The knuckles were enlarged, and there were the signs of many old fractures on the gnarled fingers.

'Can I finally get a new dress this year?' the woman asked her husband.

'I told you that you could,' he answered gruffly, but with a shallow smile.

'And maybe a little blanket for Sharon's new baby boy?' the woman went on hopefully. 'We can have some meat to eat for a change!' she said, her old eyes bright with anticipation. 'Everything's going to be fine for a while.'

'Then we can start worrying about next year,' the old man said, 'but for now, everything's fine now that we have actual money in the bank.'

The bank clerk stamped their deposit slip, and exchanging another smile, the old people turned toward the door.

Jim Early watched them as they exited, happy with their circumstances. Billy Hinton gestured toward Jim to set the procedure into motion. Jim threw up his arms and said loudly, 'Well, can you beat that, boys? I've gone and forgotten to bring my pay packet! We'll have to come back later.'

'What do you mean?' Arvin Hinton, the older of the two, asked darkly.

'Just that, I must have left my pay packet at home. We'll have to come back later.'

'You come back later,' Arvin Hinton said, pulling his pistol out. 'I intend to conduct my business now.'

Jim Early was stuck. There was nothing to do but to go along with the robbery or head for the door.

Jim headed for the door.

The Hintons didn't get away with it. The man Jim Early passed as he was exiting the bank turned out to be a deputy sheriff. Arvin and Billy were arrested on the spot, and word had it that they were hanged for their crime.

But the law had a good description of Jim, and even his name, which one of the Hintons must have provided, perhaps out of pique. That was when Jim Early became Jim Travers. Not that his attempt to hide his identity would fool anyone for long, not if he was ever taken back to Clovis; but in time the robbery became old news, and since two perpetrators had been hanged for the crime and no money was ever actually lost from the bank, the matter was all but forgotten.

Except for the gossip – with little entertainment out here, men always embellished what they knew and invented what they did not. Jim Early, therefore, was known to be a bank robber on the run and a deadly man. In some versions of the story he had escaped with the money from the bank while his unfortunate accomplices were captured. This, apparently, all due to Jim's skill with firearms, and redoubtable courage.

It did no good to try to deny these fictions, and in some places a reputation, however spurious, could be of benefit to a man. People tended to leave known badmen alone.

Zanzibar was one such place.

For the next hour while the sun rose higher and Jim perspired freely under his red shirt and blue jeans, he tramped the main street of Zanzibar on the futile hunt for the stolen money. It was useless, as he had known it would be before even beginning. Ben Lytle had stashed the money cleverly. Or he had passed it off to a trusted accomplice. It didn't matter which – it was gone.

There was nothing to do now but face the music, and so Jim started miserably back toward the Strawberry Heights Hotel where the End of Days awaited.

Along the way Jim noticed three men in town suits standing in front of Lucky's Emporium watching his progress. One of them lifted a finger and another shook his head adamantly. It didn't matter what they were saying; Jim had just provided the topic of interest for the day, nothing more.

As he approached the fancifully named white, two-story hotel, he was acutely aware of the lack of coin jingling in his jeans. He glanced up toward a second-story balcony, took a deep breath and crossed the lobby to the staircase, knowing his mettle was about to be sorely tested.

Linda Lu Finch waited in their shared room. She had managed to pry herself out of the bed in time to dress for dinner. Linda said her late sleeping was only a matter of habit and she was working to change it. She had formerly been a dancer in night spots, keeping incredibly late hours, but Jim Early, being the altruistic sort, had rescued her from that sordid life a few months back in Las Cruces.

Linda was now seated on the edge of their rumpled bed, drawing on one of her black stockings. This was not your average sight to behold; Linda Lu Finch had the longest, most well-turned legs God ever attached to a human body. Jim Early thought that if he stared at her legs long enough he might faint. These were the basis for his altruism, he later was forced to admit.

Her mouth was not yet painted as red as it would be later in the evening, and now Jim could see, as he should have noticed months earlier, that it was a pouting, sulky, spoiled little mouth. Her voice was harsh when she spoke.

'All right, Jim, where is it?'

He knew what she meant but he said, 'Where's what?'

Linda Lu rose, a stocking in one hand, the other on her hip. 'You know what I mean. Where is that fortune you were going to win today? I'm a partner in your undertakings, remember? Unwilling partner, but partner all the same, and you left with two hundred dollars of my hard-earned cash money to help stake the game.'

Jim sagged on to one of the two wooden chairs in the room, removed his hat and replied. 'Look, Linda, I've had a hard time of it already today.'

'You didn't win,' she said, still hovering over him. Jim lifted a hand and momentarily shifted his gaze to the

15

window, which showed a clear blue, long-running sky. Linda had moved nearer yet.

'I did win, Linda, I won big.'

'Well, that's something,' she said in a slightly softened voice. 'Where's the loot?'

'The thing is,' Jim said, voicing the words through a dry throat, 'I got robbed.'

'You got robbed,' Linda repeated in a dangerously low voice. 'You got robbed! Mister tough guy got himself robbed? Did the man get away?'

'No, I followed him along and shot him. He's dead,' Jim said.

'That was you shooting out in the street?' She shook her pretty head and a few dark strands draped themselves across her brown eyes. 'Well, you got the money back, then?'

'No, that's just it – he didn't have the money on him when I caught up with him.'

'That does it then, we're broke and stranded in this … pitiful little town!' Linda turned her back and let out a long sigh, which whistled through her teeth. With her back still to him, she stood staring out the window. A butcher bird perched briefly on the windowsill and Linda shooed it away with a swat of her hand.

She spun back to face him. 'Jim, I could have married a lawyer, a banker, but I had to fall for your lop-sided face and innocent blue eyes. Tell me why? I guess it was that little bit of devil-may-care swagger about you, that crooked smile. It all made you seem bold and interesting and a little dangerous.

'Well,' she continued, waving a hand around the

cramped hotel room. 'Is there anything interesting about this life we've been leading? I send out my bold man with the last bit of coin in my purse and he gets it taken from him by some local weasel. What am I supposed to do now, Jim? I can't trust you to take care of us, and I am not going back to work!'

'I wouldn't want you to,' Jim said. 'That's the reason I got you out of there in the first place. It's not right for you to have to lift your skirts and flash your legs, wearing that fake smile all the time.'

'But you didn't mind looking,' Linda said.

'I had the right,' Jim said lamely. Linda had again sunk on to the bed to put her other stocking on. Her face was sullen, the jaw muscles tight, her lips compressed.

'My fault,' Linda answered, flipping a hand in the air. 'And I was too old to believe in notions like love … my fault to fall for a man who has plenty of nothing – except for all those rocks you have in your empty head!'

'Linda, look, I am going to find that money.'

'Sure you are, and then you'll lose it in the next town – if we ever get out of this one.' Her voice had grown tauter; her words were spaced out in angry segments. She flung away the pink silk wrapper she had been wearing and walked to the closet to look for a dress.

'It'll work out, Linda. Honest. I'll find that money.'

'I am not going back to work!' she shouted, although he hadn't mentioned that as a possibility.

'Of course not.'

'Why do you think I went along with you? I was so sick of that life.' She was fastening the small buttons on the front of a shiny green dress with black lace at the cuffs and collar. There must have been over fifty buttons. Her fingers worked nimbly, used to the chore.

Looking into the mirror as she pinned her hair up, she asked, 'What else did you manage to bollix up? You haven't paid the livery bill yet. Did you sell my horse and buggy for ready cash?'

'Don't be silly. All I did was—'

'All you did,' she said in a hiss, bending toward him, both hands on her hips, 'was empty my purse to stake your gambling, lose the money and kill a man in the street. A busy day so far; I guess you didn't have the time to do much more to strand us here.'

'Linda, I didn't—' There was a sharp rap of knuckles on the door, interrupting him. Both turned their eyes that way.

'What's that?' Linda asked sourly. 'Another chicken come home to roost? No, I guess not, nothing else could go wrong, could it?'

'I don't know,' Jim muttered, and he crossed to the door to open it. Three men in gray suits stood there. The tallest of the three smiled nervously and said:

'Jim Travers, we've come to offer you the position of town marshal.'

TWO

'What did he say?' Linda asked excitedly. 'He's the marshal? Now the town law has come after you for killing a man?' Her look was one of disgust.

'I said,' the unidentified man told her with a lingering gaze, 'that we have come to offer Jim the position of town marshal of Zanzibar.'

Linda Lu roared with surprised laughter. The three men in the doorway frowned. 'May we come in?' their spokesman inquired.

'Sure, come on in,' Jim said, glancing at Linda, who was concentrating on her shoe buttons. 'Excuse me, gentlemen, I just wasn't aware that it was April Fools' Day already.'

'I assure you. . . .' their leader, a narrow man with a slightly hooked nose and full lips, said. He looked around for places to sit. There was only one other chair besides Linda's and he took the chair himself, leaving the other two men hovering in the background like gray-suited vultures.

'I am Mayor Hazlitt,' the man told Jim, who was surprised to learn that Zanzibar had such a thing as a mayor. No one had told him that before. 'And these gentlemen are Peter Wiley and Frank Gerard, two members of the city council. I know,' Hazlitt said, lifting a hand, 'you were not even aware that Zanzibar had such a structure. Actually it is a fairly new arrangement.'

'A week ago, Tuesday,' the man who had been introduced as Peter Wiley said. He was a broad-faced, well-rounded man with a look of sincerity. Hazlitt glanced at him sharply. It was Hazlitt's show in his mind.

Linda Lu was pinning her hat on. The men's eyes frequently drifted that way.

'You see, Mister Travers, Zanzibar has been pretty rough and tumble up until now. Many of our local citizens are of unknown origin and uncertain character. You must have noticed this?' Jim only nodded, slightly amused, but wondered if there was something in this that he could turn to his advantage. Linda Lu was painting her lips bright, bright red. Hazlitt cleared his throat, drew his gaze away from her, and continued.

'You see, we have it in mind to let Zanzibar progress along the road to civilization, to put a new face on the town, as it were,' he said, perhaps still thinking of Linda Lu's applications of powder and paint.

'We seldom get the right kind of people wanting to move here; the kind who want a settled town with churches and schools for their kids. We are only a rough, dusty trail town and we want to change that.

'People come through here and before they have

even viewed the charm and understood the advantages of moving to Zanzibar, why, they're gone.'

'I'm going now,' Linda Lu announced to everyone. She picked up her tote, shouldered it, and walked past the men with a flounce of skirts and the waft of rose scent. She closed the door sharply behind her. With a pained look on his face, Hazlitt looked at Jim, who told them:

'It wasn't your company – she does this all the time. She'll be back.' He was not so certain of that, though; not this time. Outside of catching her and tying her up, however, he could not do a thing about it. He returned his attention to the mayor and town councilmen.

'I get this from what you've told me – you want to clean up the town, make it a safe place for business and families. You still haven't said why you're here. What makes you think I'd want a job as town marshal? More, what makes you think I'd be any good at it?'

'Just today you demonstrated integrity and good judgment,' the third man, Frank Gerard, who wore a big red walrus mustache, said.

'I did?' Jim said with surprise. 'When was that? A man robbed me in the Red Bird and I went after him.'

'Because he had committed a crime!' Wiley said.

'And when you did catch up with him, you didn't just shoot him down out of hand. You returned fire only when your own life was threatened.'

Jim smiled faintly. Let them read into the episode whatever they wanted. For one thing he had not been truly afraid of the little pea-shooter Ben Lytle had been armed with. Those little short-barreled guns would do the job across a poker table, but at any range at all they were just about useless. However, Lytle was doing his best to kill him. Jim shrugged away the faint praise.

'All I really had in mind was getting the money back. The little rat had stashed it somewhere, or more likely handed it off to another man as he ran.'

'You mean to continue looking for the money, don't you?' Frank Gerard said from under his huge mustache.

'I do,' Jim said flatly.

'Yes, I imagine having it would mean a lot to your young lady.'

'I imagine it would – a part of it was hers!'

Mayor Hazlitt looked sympathetic. 'Yes, I know it's hard to disappoint a woman, especially where money is concerned.'

'I'll get it back,' Jim vowed.

'Yes,' Peter Wiley said, 'but that might prove a little thorny, mightn't it?'

'Whereas,' Hazlitt said as a man who has heard his cue, 'if you were a marshal wearing a silver shield, you'd likely encounter less opposition in your pursuit.'

'You'd be free to question any suspect under the cloak of authority,' Gerard commented.

Jim stared at the three of them for a moment before he smiled grimly and said, 'That would be a hell of a reason to take up law enforcement, especially in a rugged town like Zanzibar.'

'I, myself, keep thinking of the young lady – what is her name?'

'Linda Finch,' Jim muttered.

'Yes. A fine-looking woman. She's obviously not happy with you, seeing that you have no means of supporting her now,' Hazlitt said as if considering. 'We haven't yet discussed the budgeting for the new office of town marshal, but I think we can promise you that it would be enough to support a man and his wife.'

'She's not my wife,' Jim growled.

Hazlitt shrugged with one shoulder. 'To support a couple, shall we say, then?'

'After you recover your poker winnings, if you choose to resign your office and move on,' Gerard said, 'we would understand and respect your decision.'

'You still haven't said enough to convince me that I belong behind a badge,' Jim said, 'not even half enough.'

'Oh, all right, then!' Hazlitt said, showing irritation. 'Peter Wiley has not been in town long – well, none of has. Peter, will you tell Mr Travers where you are from, and what you were doing?'

Peter Wiley glanced at Jim Travers, briefly toward the window where the butcher bird had returned, and back. The broad-faced man's amiable smile was directed at no one.

'Well, you see, I moved up here a while back from Clovis, New Mexico.'

'Did you ever have occasion to see Mr Travers down there?' Mayor Hazlitt asked.

'Only once,' Wiley said as Jim's stomach began to tighten. 'Some men, there were three of them, tried to rob the bank down there. Two of them were caught and hanged.' He wagged his head. 'The third man got away.

23

I suppose they must still be looking for him. But you know these outlaws; they have a way of hiding right under the noses of the law.'

So it was blackmail, then? Jim was thinking. He was also thinking that the other points the three men had raised made sense. He was not going to survive long on what he had in his jeans and Linda was certain to run away if they lost their hotel room and their possibilities. He could not really blame her. And a man with some authority did have a better chance of asking questions that would be answered and discovering where the stolen money was.

It went hard against the grain, but as Jim looked into the faces of the three men whose eyes had gone stony in the interim, he gave them the only answer that would satisfy them, the only answer that he could give under the circumstances.

'So pin your badge on me, men. I'm the new marshal of Zanzibar.'

At least he would eat. The mayor had handed him a twenty-dollar gold piece as an advance on his salary after pinning the silver badge on to Jim's shirt. He had taken an oath, which he could see they meant to have him adhere to, and signed an agreement drawn up by the town judge, a man named O'Connell. He'd seen them out of the hotel room and slipped a leather vest over his red shirt, hoping that the vest concealed the shiny contours of the badge, which must have been made very recently, especially for the town.

Jim went out, feeling the weight of the badge, and made his way toward the hotel restaurant where he

knew that Linda Lu would be dining sumptuously, pre-
pared to charge the meal to their hotel room, knowing
that it might be her last supper for a long time. At least
Jim Early could ease that concern.

If no others.

Linda was just finishing with a roast duck served with
chestnuts and shallots. She looked pleased with herself.
Jim figured the chef, whoever he was, must have been
happy to have someone order his finest concoction. In
a town where people favored beef and potatoes without
fancy trimmings, it must have been a supreme moment
for him.

Leave it to Linda Lu.

'I thought I'd better,' she said, noticing Jim's eyes on
her platter. 'If you're going to stiff them for a meal, let
it be their finest. I'm a town girl, Jim,' she went on.
'You'd have me riding across the desert dining on
parched corn and venison if I let you.'

'No, I wouldn't,' Jim said honestly. He didn't mean
for Linda to ever suffer. She had been quite a belle
down in Las Cruces; even if her position was not
enough for the finer ladies of town to admit her into
their circles, the prominent men of Las Cruces all
enjoyed her company and were more than willing to
indulge her. He had made himself a promise to live up
to Linda's expectations as best he could – not that he
was doing that good of a job at it to this point.

'I can pay for the meal,' Jim said, placing the twenty-
dollar gold coin on the table. 'Order ice cream if you
wish.'

'They don't have it.' Linda's eyes were fixed on the

double-eagle. 'You got our money back, then?' she asked hopefully.

'Not yet. This is just an advance on wages for my new job.'

'What job?' Linda, who had a fear of manual labor and a disdain for men who did it, demanded.

'Working for the town.'

'Working for. . . ?' Linda's eyes swept across Jim, from his frank, pale-blue eyes to his amused mouth, down to his shirt where the edge of the silver badge could be seen behind the edge of his leather vest. 'My God, Jim Early!' she said, and she choked on her food. In a less public place she would have broken into a loud guffaw, but Linda had long experience at maintaining her dignified mien in public. She placed her forearms on the table, nudging her platter away, and lifted those dark-brown eyes of hers to his.

'You! A lawman? My God, Jim, do they know what you are, who you are?'

'They know too much about me,' he answered.

'But they want you as their lawman?'

'It's a rough town. I suppose their thinking is that they need someone like me – or rather like someone they think I am.'

A waitress appeared and Linda let her pour two tablespoons of coffee into her demitasse cup. Jim looked up and said, 'I'll take a mug of that if you can manage it.'

The weary waitress smiled and went off to find a full-sized cup for him.

'Where are we supposed to live?' Linda wanted to

know, sipping at her coffee. 'Until the day you're gunned down in the street, I mean.'

'That has been settled – Frank Gerard has a little house he owns where we can stay. He owns a lot of property around town. These men are Zanzibar's leading citizens, Linda. The kind you always liked rubbing elbows with.'

'In Las Cruces, maybe, but in Zanzibar?'

'All right, don't scoff. We're better off than we were this morning – and what do you mean until the day I'm gunned down in the street?'

'Just that,' she said, pausing as the waitress returned with a full-sized mug of coffee for Jim. 'Walk around town wearing that badge, getting in men's way, and it'll happen. These people plain don't want the law in Zanzibar.'

'I don't intend to knock over anyone's applecart, Linda,' Jim said seriously. 'I just want to have something for us to live on until I can find the stolen money.'

'Oh, I know you. You'll knock over someone's cart. . . . How much money did you lose, Jim?'

'I didn't lose it, it was—'

'All right, all right. How much was stolen from you – from us?' she asked.

'I wasn't keeping an exact tally,' Jim told her. 'How much did you lend me?'

'How much did you take from me?' Linda said with a deep, accusing frown.

'All right, all right! How much was yours to begin with?'

27

'You know full well. Two hundred dollars, gold money.'

'That turned into four thousand the first half-hour. Ben Lytle was too eager to build the pot up. He was a crooked dealer, but not too good at it. When I saw him make a slick move, I'd fold. I never called him on it. What was the point? When he made an outlandishly large raise, I'd get out and wait for my next hand. The man was just too desperate to win.'

Linda did not wish to hear Jim relive the entire poker game hand by hand. Thoughtfully, she bit at her lower lip and said, 'Four thousand in the first half-hour, huh?'

'Yes. The man had deep pockets for someone who kept whining about how much debt he had. He had lost something like twenty thousand before two o'clock.'

'And you let him walk away with that much! Twenty thousand?'

'I'll get it back. That's why I took this job, Linda. For the money . . . and for you.'

She wasn't totally mollified when they left the café and returned to their room, but at least her simmering anger had settled. She was not as cold to him as she could have been that night.

Still Jim Early slept uneasily. He tossed and turned, wondering what had been behind the determination of the men of Zanzibar to press the job of town marshal on him. Their reasons, when examined again, seemed flimsy.

He thought he understood a part of it – they wanted him as their legally appointed hired gun. To protect them against what? Jim knew the men of Zanzibar as well or better than they did. They were a rough bunch, but for the most part they policed themselves. After all, life in Zanzibar was preferable to life on the outlaw trail.

Wherever men collected they eventually decided to form some sort of civilized rule of life. The time had come for Zanzibar and the others in their minds.

But why Jim?

His reputation as a hard-edged gunfighter was largely unfounded. Of course the three, Mayor Hazlitt, Frank Gerard, and Peter Wiley, did not know that. As always, the men only knew what they had heard, despite the dependability of the source. Perhaps it didn't matter; as he had told Linda, they were in a better position than they had been that morning.

Jim rolled over, and as the night birds continued to sing, he let his hand search for and rest on one of Linda's too-exquisite legs.

For the moment, life was good.

By the time they had moved their few belongings into the little house on Maple Street, a dusty lane with no neighbors occupying any of the others of a row of six cottages, it was nearly sundown.

Linda Lu, wearing her favorite red dress, was seated on the single gold-colored plush chair in the bare living room, her eyes as shuttered as they could be without closing her eyelids. Jim had just finished sweeping the dust and grime from the kitchen floor out the back door. Returning, he glanced around and said, 'Well, it will take a while, but it's a start. At least we have a roof over our heads.'

'Jim,' Linda said in a distant voice, 'have you looked around this house, or outside at the brown, deprived yard, the neighbors' dry, deprived yards? Of course, there are no neighbors, so you can't blame them. Apparently everyone else has more sense than to move out this way.'

'It's not that sort of an area, Linda. Not just yet. The cottages are nice enough. It's just that men who are just passing through, the rough men, aren't looking for a place to settle down. If Zanzibar grows the way Mayor Hazlitt and the rest of the council are hoping it will, we'll soon have new neighbors, working people with kids and dogs who will care about their yards and fixing the places up.'

'Oh, glory!' Linda muttered. 'What century is that supposed to happen, Jim? I know you never promised me the moon, but I was hoping even you could find me a decent place on this planet.'

'It's not so bad,' Jim replied. He tried to perch on the arm of Linda's chair, but she refused to move her hand from it. He looked around the bare room, at the never-used fireplace, a refuge from the world that had been built in expectation of turning a profit through the influx of new citizens. Who had not arrived or not wished to put down roots in Zanzibar after having had a look at the place. It made it clearer why Frank Gerard wished the town to take a turn toward moderate. He had money and time invested in the row of cottages, and no buyers. The same applied to Peter Wiley, who owned the dry goods store in town. He couldn't make

much of a living selling goods to wandering roughnecks. They required little. Wiley also operated a
hardware store and a blacksmith's shop and owned a
handful of vacant lots. None of which appealed greatly
to Zanzibar's roaming inhabitants. And the townsfolk
had little cash money to spend. That was carefully
hoarded for major expenses such as tobacco and
alcohol.

The three men owned a large part of the town,
minus only the money-making Red Bird Saloon, which
was held by a man named Pippen. Pippen was apparently on the outs with the 'town council' over some past
dispute.

That was the situation as Jim Early understood it
from a morning conversation with Gerard, who had
taken them out to the cottage with Linda Lu driving
her buggy, and given the small house over to Jim's
charge.

'I need some money,' Linda told Jim.

'Haven't you still got the change from the restaurant?'

'Yes, I have,' she answered tightly, 'and you know it.
But look around you. How am I supposed to set up
housekeeping here with no money?' The way Linda
emphasized the word 'housekeeping' made it clear that
such a task as a permanent basis was beyond and
beneath her. Jim understood her. Linda Lu had been a
glamorous woman, used to the favors and gifts of men.
Whereas Jim Early thought they were running in luck
having the cottage given to them, to Linda Lu it was the
end of a road and all things cheerful that the world had

31

to offer. She would never be happy here, never content in a place like Zanzibar.

Jim drew her to her feet and put his arms around her. Smiling he said, 'As soon as I get our money back, we'll leave – go wherever you like. We can make out just fine on twenty thousand dollars.'

'That's fine,' she said, turning her face as Jim tried to kiss her. 'But what are we to do until then? And when will it be, Jim?'

'I'm starting tonight. I wanted to get you situated in a safe place first. I've got to find that money, and I suppose if I'm going to make any pretense of earning my wages, I'd better at least show my face around town.'

'Don't get into any trouble,' Linda said with some consternation. He looked deeply into her liquid brown eyes. Yes, she was afraid of what might happen to him, but it wasn't love.

Jim was the only hope she had for building her life again. He knew that she felt she had hitched her wagon to a falling star. Linda Lu was not the sort of woman who would ever agree to live in poverty, even as a means to an end.

His hands fell away from her shoulders. Linda tossed her hair, which was loose on this evening, and told him, 'Harness my horse to the buggy before you leave, will you? I'll be going out myself after I clean up and change clothes.'

'Out. . . ?' Jim said. 'Where will you go?'

Linda laughed. 'Why, to get something to eat, for one thing. At the hotel restaurant, one supposes. There's no other place in town I'd be seen in.'

Jim shrugged. He had been hoping without reason that she might be returning to town to buy a sack of potatoes and some meat, maybe some eggs for breakfast to cook at home. He had unrealistic expectations, he knew. He had never seen Linda even attempt to cook a thing or heard her consider the matter. Well, this wasn't the time to concern himself with that. It was time he was getting to work.

'I'll see that your bay is harnessed,' he told her, still hoping for a kiss, which he did not receive.

Linda grew briefly serious. She touched the sleeve of his shirt and said, 'Don't get yourself killed on your first night at work.'

'There's nothing to worry about there,' Jim laughed.

He was wrong, of course, as he was wrong about so many things.

Still, Linda's words provided something for Jim to mull over as he rode slowly back to Zanzibar, the sun dying in the west, splashing the thin clouds with purple and dull crimson light.

It was not the best time of day to be searching around in alleys, poking into trash cans or questioning people, but Jim had felt a strong obligation to have Linda settled somewhere before he began his search again. In the end, it made virtually no difference, Jim considered. Linda was unsatisfied. And he had no idea where to begin his hunt. He was almost ready to concede that he had already lost his prize.

In both areas.

He was baffled as to where to begin looking for the stolen money, and he had no illusions about Linda Lu.

She would not be around long if he could not come up with it. It was a moment, as he shuffled down the main street of Zanzibar, that he felt like throwing up his hands and just riding out alone on some new trail. But the new trail, whichever way he chose, would lead him nowhere at all. He had a chance here, in Zanzibar, to be something for a while. Even if it was not something he had ever wished to become.

He looked idly in every alleyway once more, his thoughts returning to the day before as he looked under porches and poked through empty crates and barrels in the darkness of the evening.

A few wagons had passed them by as he had pursued Lytle. The bag could have been tossed aboard one of those, but Jim thought he would have seen such a maneuver. No, the most likely possibility still remained that Lytle had passed off the bag to an accomplice or friend. That person, whoever it had been, knew that Lytle was now dead, and likely would have left town without delay, his fortune assured.

Up the street now, Jim could hear the sounds of the nightlife in the Red Bird. Lights flickered behind the red and blue glasses of pane as the usual rowdy crowd wandered in to celebrate . . . nothing. That was something that had occurred to Jim a long time ago: lonely, beaten men congregated in these saloons. Spending money they could ill afford to celebrate . . . absolutely nothing.

With his confidence in this project waning, Jim entered one more dank, dark alleyway running between the dry goods store and a saddlery. He had barely taken four strides toward a loading dock belonging to the dry goods store when the alley flared with light and the sound of gunshots.

Jim Early dove toward the cover of the loading dock, pawing at his own pistol, trying to slip it as bullets whined off the side of the dock, off the face of the building. Abruptly, the shooting stopped as a few men shouting came rushing toward the head of the alley.

The echoes of the gunshots lingered in Jim's ears. The remnants of gunsmoke still hung in the air. But the shooter, whoever he was, had not wanted to stick around to finish the job with so many witnesses arriving on the scene.

Someone called out, 'What's going on? Who's in there?'

'Jim Travers!' Jim called back, and he heard a soft murmuring, felt their interest ebb. Why was that? The crowd dispersed, returning to the Red Bird. Jim stood, dusted off his trousers, and picked up his hat. A lone, narrow figure remained at the head of the alley as Jim looked over his shoulder in the direction the shooter had gone, and he walked that way.

'Glad you men showed up,' Jim said to the man he recognized but did not know. He thought his name was Tibbs, Bernie Tibbs. They had brushed elbows in the saloon and discussed trivial matters like the weather and quality of the Red Bird's drinks. 'It didn't take long for people to clear out. I thought they'd be more interested.'

They usually were; any bit of excitement sustained men for a long while in this town and other towns like it. They had practically flocked around him when he had shot Lytle the day before.

'It's just that once they knew who you were, they kinda lost interest,' Bernie Tibbs said vaguely.

Jim frowned. In the meager light he could see the narrow, dark-eyed man's face. A crop of dark whiskers, narrow mouth and long chin. It was not a happy face.

'I don't understand you,' Jim said. 'I never had any trouble with anyone in town.'

'Up until now,' Tibbs said. He made a gesture toward the badge Jim wore on his shirt.

'Now, I'd guess you can expect nothing but trouble – and damned little sympathy.'

'Come on, Tibbs, I'll buy you a drink,' Jim Early said. 'I want to tell you something. There's only one reason I have for wearing this badge on my shirt – I mean to have back the money that Ben Lytle stole from me.'

'That doesn't make a lot of sense to me,' Tibbs said as they made their way toward the Red Bird.

'No, I guess it wouldn't,' Jim admitted. 'But it's true, and I'm stuck if I can't recover it. I had every nickel I have riding on that poker game.'

'All I know,' Tibbs told him, 'is that if you had shot the skunk down in the Red Bird, men would have stuck by you stronger than they will now that you have run off and pinned a badge on for that greedy little kingdom-builder, Hazlitt. Or should I say "Mayor Hazlitt"? Who voted for him, anyway? And when was the election held? I have no idea.'

Bernie Tibbs halted in the middle of the dark street, glancing toward the Red Bird.

'Hazlitt has it in mind to get rid of the Red Bird and all of us saddletramps. Do you think Colin Pippen will stand for that?'

'I don't know Pippen. I met him once, nodded to him a few more times but I don't think he should be worried. No one is going to shut down the Red Bird. Why should they?'

'There's bad blood between Pippen and Hazlitt and the others anyway. I don't know all of it, but it's certain that Pippen is making more money than anyone in Zanzibar, and Hazlitt can't stomach it. And you – you're just Hazlitt's hired gun, Jim. Everyone in the Red Bird will be against you trying to upset things.'

'I don't want to upset anything!' Jim insisted. 'I just want to find out where my money has gotten to.'

'It ain't me that you have to convince,' Tibbs said with a shake of his head. 'I was just telling you how things seem to everyone else. And,' he touched Jim's arm lightly, 'don't think Pippen will stand for it. He knows a lot of people, and he's likely to hire a few who are good with their guns.'

Bernie Tibbs spun away, insisting that he could find a way to get his own drinks. Jim watched the thin man saunter off, wondering what he had gotten himself into now. Jim had a couple of dollars in his pocket, but he didn't think that now was the time to visit the Red Bird if the local men were as worked up as Tibbs had indicated.

They had had all day to drink and discuss matters among themselves and apparently animosity was building against the man they had decided wanted to close down their refuge – the Red Bird Saloon.

Jim's stomach reminded him that he was hungry. By now Linda would have driven herself to the hotel restaurant, and Jim decided they could not afford two of the fancy dinners there, so he walked back up the street, deep in thought, trudging toward the only other place he knew to eat in town, Ethel M's restaurant.

Jim started that way, thinking that it might not be a bad idea to have a talk with Colin Pippen, the owner of the Red Bird Saloon, when he could. He had no idea what was going on with the local politics, and Pippen seemed to be right in the middle of it all. Jim had only the word of Mayor Hazlitt – might as well call him that – and the others as to what the situation was in Zanzibar. Pippen might have a totally different point of view, and maybe he would be willing to talk to Jim before he blundered into a situation he was not expecting.

Would Pippen be at his saloon on this night? It didn't really matter. Jim did not think that with the men drinking as heavily as they were it was a good time to visit there.

Approaching the alleyway before that which bordered Ethel M's restaurant, he decided to walk its length once again – there may have been something he had missed. He doubted it, but if he was going to search, then make it as thorough as he could. He sauntered along slowly through the darkness; to a casual eye it would appear that it was aimless wandering, but Jim's eyes were alert for every deep shadow, bit of refuse, possible hiding place.

There was nothing to be found.

At the end of the alley he stood for a moment, looking toward the corral standing on a grassy, open field shaded by black oak trees. There most of the horses belonging to the wandering men of Zanzibar were being held. The sheltered stable and sacked grain the animals fed on were too expensive for most of the men Jim knew, those who had to carefully watch their pocket coin so that they did not run short of whiskey money.

And where would these men go when their money had run out? To find more money, of course. Were most of them roving outlaws? Jim felt sure that they were, in one small way or another, from conversations they had had with him. Were these the threats to Zanzibar that Mayor Hazlitt wanted so badly to send packing? Probably, although the men, rowdy as they could be, seemed reluctant to start anything that would foul their own nest.

Jim walked along past the rear of Ethel M's and entered the narrow darkness of the alley beside it. There, too, he looked at or searched the standing rubbish, even peering into a few garbage cans, rattling their lids as he closed them again.

On a side porch of the restaurant he saw a slender figure working away at a tedious job. Behind the worker the kitchen door stood ajar an inch or so, offering a narrow band of light to see by. The worker was busy in her work, scraping the dishes off into a garbage pail with a butter knife, not seeing his slow approach.

Jim halted for a minute to watch her, for he could

now see the worker was a slender blonde girl, no more than twenty years old. Her face was intent on her task, but she suddenly saw or felt Jim's presence. She looked up sharply, her eyes cold in the feeble light shining through the restaurant window.

'What are you looking at?' she demanded, halting in her task.

'Nothing – just wondered what you were doing back here,' Jim said.

'What I'm doing, mister, is sitting behind a restaurant, scraping the garbage from the dishes before I wash them. What is it that you usually do with your dirty dishes?'

Her voice was mocking, but not really unpleasant. Jim laughed and answered, 'I don't know, I really haven't had that many dishes to take care of except when I'm on the trail. Then I just scrub them out with a little sand or let them wait.'

'You live in town now,' the girl said. 'Is that what you do here?'

Jim thought. 'I really haven't had any dirty dishes since I got here.'

'What do you do, lick them clean?' she asked.

'Just about. I meant that I've been doing all my eating in restaurants.'

'All of it? Gets a little expensive, doesn't it?'

'Yes, it does.'

'Don't you have a house yet?' the girl asked, lowering the dish she had been scraping.

'I do,' Jim told her. 'But it doesn't have any dishes yet.'

'That's the first thing to purchase, mister.'

'Yes, I suppose it is.' Jim shrugged, removed his hat and wiped back his hair, stepping nearer. The girl watched him with curiosity but not timidity. That was good; he didn't like to think of himself as an intimidating sort of man.

'Wait a minute!' the girl said. 'I know who you are now. I've seen you before – your name's Jim something.'

'Jim Travers,' he provided.

'Yes, I know you,' she said, bending forward to peer at Jim's face. 'You're the one who squires around that fancy woman.'

'I don't think she'd care for that description,' Jim said to the blonde.

'I'll bet not! But I don't know what else you'd call her with all those fancy dresses and jewels, her hair done up so pretty. There's never been a woman like that in the town of Zanzibar before.'

Jim was not going to apologize or explain to the blonde girl. Linda Lu was just Linda Lu.

'Wait a minute,' the blonde said, rising to her feet, holding the scraping knife beside her aproned thigh. 'You're wearing a badge!'

'That's right,' Jim said, fingering it rather self-consciously, 'I'm the marshal of Zanzibar.'

'The marshal of. . . ? Mister, you surely are a sudden man!'

'Not really,' Jim said. 'I don't think I know what you mean.'

'I know a few other things about you now that I've

had the time to put them all together. You're the man who came into town with this fancy woman, wins a fortune at the card tables from Ben Lytle, shoots him dead in the street, and lives in one of those cottages owned by Frank Gerard out there,' she said, gesturing with the knife. 'And now, here you are, the town marshal.' She laughed. 'And, mister, you're saying you're not the sudden sort!'

'When you put it that way, it does sound a little rapid, I'll admit.'

'Rapid? Mister, compared to the other men in town you are a tornado! Most of them over at the Red Bird, you'd have to prod 'em with a stick to get them to as much as move from their bar stools.'

'Things just happened to me,' Jim explained. 'I had to go along with them or be left alongside the trail.'

'Well, well,' the girl said, still studying him speculatively. 'And what do I call you in the event I ever happen to need the law, which might be real soon?'

'Marshal Travers. Or just Jim, whichever makes you comfortable.' He frowned. 'What makes you think that you may have trouble on the way?'

'Mister,' she said, shaking her head, 'everyone in this hellhole of a town has trouble at their doorsteps or on the way. Maybe I'll tell you about it sometime,' she said as she bent to pick up the heavy tray of dishes. 'Where would that be – where I can have a conversation with you, I mean?'

Jim hesitated and laughed. 'I don't really know. The mayor, no one, has given me an office yet.'

'That's the kind of a mess you can get into when you

move too sudden, Jim,' the blonde replied. Then she returned to the restaurant kitchen, nudging the door open with her hip as she swung the tray of dishes inside and disappeared.

Strange. Well, it had been a strange day. Jim wanted only to eat and ride back to the cottage.

He walked toward the front door of the Ethel M's restaurant and paused for a minute to peer inside, hoping that he might find Linda Lu there. Of course it was a futile hope. Would Linda ever eat at a place that boasted thirty-five-cent dinners?

Pushing in through the door, Jim found the place busy but not crowded. The warm, steamy smells and feel of the place were welcome to a cold, hungry man. Ethel M's suited him just fine. He could remember very well the days when he wandered with the Hinton brothers, catching a meal wherever they could, usually on the open desert. In those days, this small restaurant would have seemed like a bit of heaven.

Jim seated himself, placing his hat on the table. As he waited, he glanced around the room and was surprised to find himself surrounded by a sea of hostile faces. At the tables sat rough men, most of whom he had known, joked with, played cards with, drunk raw whiskey with.

Now they turned stony eyes on him or looked away as they met his gaze. A pair of men, Junior Weber and Tyler Hough, rose from their table and walked deliberately from the restaurant as Jim seated himself. The word had gotten around, whatever it was that was now being said, and Jim Early Travers was no one's friend in this town; not anymore.

He was a man who had moved too sudden for Zanzibar.

THREE

After a heavy, fleshy woman had poured Jim a cup of coffee he sat back and waited, trying to pay no attention to those around him. It was only minutes later that a younger waitress appeared at his table, menu in her hand. He knew her. It was the blonde from the rear of the restaurant.

'You sure get around,' he said to the girl, who now wore a black skirt under a white apron and a pleasant if hesitant smile.

'You've got to keep on the move around here,' she said, her smile fading.

A man Jim did not recognize walked toward the door and called back, 'Thanks, Ginnie! See you again. Stay out of trouble.'

'That's your name – Ginnie?' Jim asked.

'I thought I told you out back. Virginia Cummings. What'll you have, Marshal?'

'Recommend something, I'm not fussy.'

'But plenty hungry?'

'Plenty.'

'I'll fix you up,' Ginnie Cummings promised, then she picked up the menu and scurried off to other tables where men were calling for her. Jim caught a good view of her reverse side, finding it pleasant. Slender, but not boyishly so, she was an attractive young woman.

When Ginnie returned with platters of roast beef, potatoes with dark gravy, corn on the cob and a wedge of apple pie, she asked, 'Figured out where you're going to conduct business yet?'

'I'll have to talk to the mayor before I find that out.'

'All right,' Ginnie said, 'be expecting me.'

This time he could see a hint of anxiety in her blue eyes, a tightness around her mouth. The girl did have some sort of problem, though what it could be Jim could not guess. He fell to eating with an appetite.

When Jim arrived back at the cottage he was not surprised to see that Linda Lu had not yet returned. The idea made him unhappy, but as he stepped inside to light the lantern and look around the empty room, he could not really blame her. What did she have to come home to?

Linda had enough money left to spend another night in the Strawberry Heights Hotel, and that was undoubtedly what she had decided to do. Still, it could cause a man an amount of concern, even though Jim knew that Linda was going to do what she damned well pleased no matter what he thought.

Once he was settled into this job and had filled the cottage with nice furniture, she would want to stay home and do womanly things. If she did not, Jim decided, by then he would have recovered his stolen money and could take her to wherever she wished to be with enough cash to support the lifestyle she preferred. There was really nothing to worry about.

He took his lone blanket from his bedroll and stretched out on the floor after blowing the lantern out. It was not a cold night although he could have wished for a second blanket – or for Linda to warm him. Why would she wish to spend the night on the hard floor? She was better off staying at the hotel for the night, until he could get things better organized for her.

Jim closed his eyes. As weary as he was, his mind continued to spin, making immediate sleep impossible. Where could his money have gotten to? And just who was it who had taken it into his mind to shoot at him in that dark alley?

He thought briefly of Ginnie Cummings and had to smile. After scraping dishes in the alley she had returned to wait on tables inside. He had noticed the cuffs of her blue jeans showing beneath the hem of the black skirt she was wearing. It seemed she was doing a little of everything at Ethel M's, and apparently doing it well from the compliments Jim had overheard others making.

What sort of trouble could the girl have? Enough for her to ask the marshal – him – for help with it?

Jim sat up sharply about an hour later. He thought he had heard someone moving around at the back of the house. He frowned, reaching for his Colt. Had Linda come home? No, he would have heard her horse and buggy, and there was no reason for her to prowl around in back when the front door was unlocked.

He started to rise, but the night had grown cooler and he was warm in his bed, and anyway, the sounds had ceased. Probably a stray dog or a roving coyote looking for garbage. There was none to be had, of course. And there was none to be found at the other cottages, all of which stood vacant.

It was, Jim reflected, a lonely sort of place to bring a woman, but it was the only place offered at the time. Jim had accepted it as a stroke of luck, no matter what Linda thought. She would come around in time. Letting that thought comfort him, Jim did finally fall back to sleep.

Morning brought no sign of Linda Lu. Of course, Jim thought as he surveyed the coloring eastern sky from the back porch, it was far too early for her to rise. Although, he had hoped. . . .

He retrieved a small sack of ground coffee and his camp-fire pot from his saddle-bags and started a fire in the black iron stove. There was water to be had from the well in the back yard. Crossing to it, Jim searched the ground for tracks – man tracks or animal tracks – but his night visitor had left none that were visible.

As the coffee boiled Jim recovered three crumbling salt biscuits from his goods and munched on one of them. It was all very much as if he had made a trail camp inside of the cottage, he thought wryly. The sky lost its color and the day began slowly to warm, and Jim gulped down his coffee and decided to get moving. There was much to do, but most of it was ill-defined.

Talk to Linda, find the mayor, and ask him about an office and jail. Try to talk with Colin Pippen at the Red

Bird. Consider asking around about who might have attempted to kill him the previous night, although chances of finding out seemed remote. Recover his missing money!

He started toward the town again, his gray horse lazily walking the distance. He would have to purchase feed for the animal and have it taken out to the cottage, lay in at least a short larder of food to sustain them for a while.

And buy some dishes. He recalled Ginnie telling him that was the first thing he should be doing. What did Jim know about setting up house? He had never attempted it before, nor had Linda Lu.

The trouble was, he had no money left to do any of these things just now. And somewhere ahead in the town of Zanzibar, there was a man sleeping comfortably with twenty thousand of Jim's dollars in his possession.

Remedying that was of prime importance, but first things first, and on consideration Jim decided that his first priority on that clear, cool morning was to find Mayor Hazlitt and have a frank talk with him. He wondered if he dared ask the man for another loan when he had been on the job exactly one night.

He walked the gray down the main street, which was nearly deserted at this early hour. He glanced at the Strawberry Heights Hotel, knowing that Linda was sleeping away comfortably and that it would only irritate her to be roused. There was a man who was vaguely familiar sitting on a tilted-back wooden chair on the hotel porch, taking the sun. Bearded, young-old looking, he watched Jim's passing with unusual attentiveness, but then Jim had managed to become a character of interest almost overnight.

Glancing across the street he looked at Ethel M's. The restaurant was open, of course, but Ginnie would not be working in the morning as well as the evening, would she? Maybe so, but Jim had no excuse to drop in and no money to eat with.

He was not even sure why he wished to see the young blonde again. Perhaps because she had indicated a need for his help. Perhaps not.

Jim eyed the street, the alleyways, as he walked his horse along. Maybe he had missed something obvious in his previous searches, though no hiding place made itself obvious on this morning either. No – he was now convinced that Ben Lytle must have passed the green bag off to a friend or acquaintance. He tried to remember the faces of the men Lytle had brushed past, but could not. His attention had been too focused on Lytle himself as the little rat made his dash from the Red Bird.

Jim left his gray horse at the Joker Stable. The man working there asked for payment in advance, but Jim brazened it out. He tapped the badge on his shirt and said that the town council would be paying his bill. He did not know if that was true or not, but the stableman, grumbling, accepted his word for it and led the gray away. Fine, Jim was thinking, now if they don't come through for me, I'm liable to lose my pony as well.

Jim had never thought long or hard about money in his life; it had never been that important to him. There was always grass for the horse, a dollar to be made here and there. But, he reflected, times had changed. There was the horse, and there was the need for food and furnishings. There was Linda, who had never gone a day in her life without instantly having whatever it was that she wished for. And Jim was not the man to provide it. Her rescuer, indeed! He was sure that she had been much happier flashing her legs for the men in Las Cruces than she was now despite her complaints. In retrospect, it might have seemed like the high point of her life.

Deciding to again retrace the route he and Lytle had taken, futile though it seemed, Jim began walking along the plank walk. The first person he met along the way was Peter Wiley, the businessman and member of the town council.

The rosy-faced Wiley was trying his best to look his usual cheerful self, but as he waved to a passing merchant and turned his eyes to Jim, the happiness washed from his face. He paused and stood waiting for Jim to approach him as he stood in the narrow band of shade cast by the awning in front of his emporium. His smile returned as Jim reached him and the two shook hands.

'Good morning . . . Marshal.'

'Good morning, Wiley. Listen, can you tell me where I could find Mayor Hazlitt at this time of the morning? I have a few things to ask him.'

'Oh?' Wiley looked surprised and preoccupied at once.

'Yes, for one thing I need to know where my office is supposed to be. People have told me that they wanted to discuss matters with me, and I have no idea where I'm supposed to have them call, nor what is going to be done about providing me with a jail.'

'You're going to arrest someone?' Peter Wiley asked nervously.

'Well, not now, but it's bound to come up eventually, don't you think? It's usual to have a town jail most places I've been.'

'I suppose we didn't give this whole project enough thought,' Wiley said, his eyes shifting away from Jim's. 'As a matter of fact, some of us are wondering if we've made the right decision in hiring you at all, Travers.'

'Some of you. . . ?' Jim's eyes narrowed. 'You people had better make up your minds what you want. What could have changed overnight to make you regret this?'

'It's just that. . . .' Wiley turned Jim away from the front door of his business to allow a town-dressed man and a lady in a blue dress to enter the store. In a lower voice, he said to Jim, 'It's nothing you've done, you understand?'

'No, I don't understand.'

'It's just . . . you know where I'm from, don't you, Jim?'

'You told me you had just arrived from Clovis.'

'Yes, that's just it,' Wiley said. He wasn't perspiring, but looked as if he would like to.

'And you've decided you don't want a man for marshal who's been implicated in the bank robbery down there?' Jim said. 'Well, let me tell you all about that episode, Wiley. I had nothing at all to do with it, though I was accused by those who did.'

'That's just it,' Wiley said for about the third time. 'I went out for breakfast early this morning, as is my habit. I happened to see two men lounging in front of the

Strawberry Heights Hotel.' He took in a full breath and said: 'It was the Hinton brothers, Travers.'

'It can't have been!' Jim said.

'I ought to know them. I was at their trial.'

'But they were hanged for the bank robbery.'

'Who told you that?'

'Why, you did, Mr Wiley.'

'I must have been trying to encourage you by making the tale more . . . dramatic. I can't recall now why I might have said that. What I meant was that they *could* have been hanged, but they weren't. Because no one was hurt during the robbery and they had no money on them when they were arrested, the judge gave them only five years' hard labor for the crime. Apparently they've served their time and are out now.'

'But why here?' Jim asked. He was thinking back to the man he had seen lounging in front of the hotel that morning. He had looked so familiar, and now he knew why. He was a ringer for Billy Hinton, had Billy ever grown a beard.

'I don't know. We – Hazlitt, Frank Gerard, and I – believe they must have come hunting for you because you ran out on them back in Clovis. It's rumored around town that you took off with the bank money and left them to pay the piper.'

'That's untrue!' Jim said vehemently. 'If there was any money missing, they ought to be looking more closely at the banker. I took nothing.'

'That may be so,' Wiley said. Now he was perspiring, mopping at his face with a folded handkerchief. 'I believe you if you say so, but you know how rumors spread.'

Did he not! Especially in Zanzibar. He said, 'But if anyone should know that I haven't got the money, it's Billy and Arvin.'

'Maybe that's so,' Wiley agreed, 'but I've asked around. The two were at the Red Bird last night and they vowed to avenge themselves because you left them to do five-year sentences in the territorial prison while you got yourself a fancy woman.' Jim started to object, but Wiley rushed on with his words.

'And the loose lips at the Red Bird apparently told the Hintons that you had won twenty thousand dollars at a poker table.'

'Yes, and promptly had it stolen from me!'

'They may have been told that,' Hinton said, 'and they may have chosen not to believe it. Either way, from what I heard, they left the saloon still angry and determined to have your hide.'

Jim grumbled a few words that Wiley couldn't make out concerning Clovis and the Hinton brothers. Then more forcefully, 'All because I did the right thing for once in my life.'

'Be that as it may,' Wiley said as two more customers passed them and entered the store, 'you can see why we're beginning to have doubts about our course of action in hiring you. That is, you have brought more trouble with you. Instead of calming the town down, you have become the instigator of more possible violence on the streets. The exact opposite of what we hoped hiring you would achieve.'

'Is that so?' Jim asked. He was fuming now, but he managed to keep his voice under control. 'Look, Wiley, I am not here to cause any trouble. If the Hinton brothers are, well, I'll have to see to that as I would with any other troublemakers. You're never going to clean up Zanzibar if you men can't make up your minds and decide on a firm path, staying the course. You want to fire your town marshal because he has had dealings in the past with a couple of roughnecks? Tell me how that makes any sense?'

Wiley sputtered something, but made no response. He looked around as if wishing for the help of his firmer council members. Governing a town seemed to be beyond his skills and desires.

Jim said, 'All I need from you right now is for you to tell me where I can find Mayor Hazlitt. It's obvious we have a few things to talk about. Have you forgotten that you three offered me, nearly forced upon me, an agreement, and I have taken an oath to do this job? That is, I'm legally bound to it. I can't be dismissed on a whim; reneging on that contract would have financial consequences for you and the others. I'm sure your Judge O'Connell could explain it to you.

'If the Hintons start trouble in Zanzibar, I will stop it if I can. That is what you men have hired me to do, and that is what I intend to do.'

FOUR

Mayor Hazlitt was surprised if not shocked to look up and see Jim enter his feed and grain store. He ducked down behind a stack of grain sacks as if he were a hunted man. Jim had seen him and he walked to the counter and waited patiently until the mayor had no choice but to re-emerge.

'Dropped something,' Hazlitt mumbled, dusting off the knees of his pants. Jim made no response and so Hazlitt went on with, 'This is unexpected. What brings you here, Travers?'

'My job,' Jim answered quietly. 'Do you want to talk out here?' There were three or four men, obviously cattle ranchers, moving around the store. Another was walking out the front door with a sack of oats, which he tossed into the back of a wagon, returning for another.

'I'll talk here, of course!' Hazlitt said congenially. The narrow, hooked-nosed man smiled, his thick lips parting to show stained teeth. 'Now, what's this about your job, Marshal?'

'I've already talked to Peter Wiley,' Jim advised the man.

'Oh . . . all right then, maybe we should be talking in my office,' Hazlitt said. He called to a man who was sweeping the floor. 'Willie, will you watch the counter for a while? Follow me, Marshal,' Hazlitt said, inclining his head.

Jim followed the mayor into a small, neat cubicle, undecorated and unfurnished except for a shabby old desk with a leather upholstered chair behind it and a wooden chair opposite. 'Sit down, Jim.'

'I won't be here that long,' Jim answered. 'I just came to tell you that you can't get rid of me this easy. You men came looking for me; I never sought the job out.' He held up a hand to still Hazlitt's comment and continued.

'You pressed a contract on me and I signed it. I took an oath. I did these things because I wanted to stay in Zanzibar until I could recover my stolen money – you know that. And, I have to have a way to take care of my woman financially while we're here.'

'You don't understand,' Hazlitt said, wearing a look of concern now.

'I do. You three want to run Zanzibar, and you want to do it well. You can't do that if you're going to second guess yourselves on every move you make. You wanted a marshal; you found one. You can't turn around the next day and fire him because you think you might have made a mistake. Is that the way you intend to run the town, making decisions, changing them on a whim? People won't give that sort of government any loyalty – they can't.'

'Events change so rapidly, Jim.'

'Sure they do. One thing that hasn't changed is that I have a contract with the town, signed by all three of you. It had better be fulfilled or I'll make my next stop a visit to Judge O'Connell.'

'Why, O'Connell would never—' Hazlitt stopped in mid-sentence, knowing that Jim had a good claim against the three men, which could cost them much money with no satisfaction obtained. Then they would have to set about trying to find another marshal – if anyone in Zanzibar would take the job. The mayor tried to explain:

'It was when these two convicts rode into town. We just wanted to avoid a confrontation in the streets. How would that look to the citizens of Zanzibar?'

'I couldn't say, but one way or the other they would know that they at least have law in this town. I can't guess what the Hinton brothers might get up to, but I know them well enough – I won't back down from them, Mayor, whether I'm wearing a badge or not.'

'I see.' Hazlitt looked at Jim with speculation. Finally he nodded. 'All right, then. We were too hasty in our response, Jim. You're still our marshal.'

'Which brings us to the next points,' Jim said. Hazlitt blinked stupidly at him. Jim explained. 'I have to have an office – I've already had citizens asking me where they could get hold of me when they had problems.' That was almost true, except that he was using the plural for Ginnie Cummings – and what was her trouble?

'An office,' Hazlitt said dully. 'Of course you need an office. Right here on Main Street would be the best site. Then visitors will know that we have law in Zanzibar!' The mayor brightened. 'I'll see what we can do, Jim. Frank Gerard has a few empty buildings along the street, waiting for new businessmen who never arrived.'

'You own a blacksmith's shop too, don't you?' Jim asked.

'Well, Peter Wiley does, if that's what you meant,' the mayor replied, his frown returning. 'Why do you ask?'

'Wherever you decide my office should be it has to have a jail attached for me to keep men in – or do you just want me to deliver them to you after I catch them?'

Hazlitt didn't catch Jim's quick smile, but he understood all too well. This was beginning to run into money. Well, it was what they had decided the town needed. There was no stopping now.

'I'll talk to Frank Gerard and then let Jan Kesselring take a look at the building and see if it's suitable for a jail – he's the town smith. I doubt he's ever taken on a job like this before, but he's a clever man with his tools.'

'Fine,' Jim said, turning toward the office door. 'I think that about does it for now, although you might want to have a carpenter paint a shingle and hang it in front of the office. No sense in trying to keep it a secret.'

'No, no there isn't,' the mayor agreed. 'I'm glad we had this talk,' he said as they walked out together. 'What do you have planned for this day?'

'I'm going to get the other side of things. Don't you think I should?'

'I don't know what you mean,' Hazlitt said haltingly.

'I intend to talk with Colin Pippen and find out why he thinks you three are planning on taking over the town and shutting down the Red Bird.'

Hazlitt was speechless for a moment, then he said shakily, 'It's not Pippen or his saloon we are fighting against – although I do wish he could move his enterprise to some other part of town, off Main Street. Some of the bums that hang around there – yes, they are bums – have been there for months, even years, doing nothing but drinking and gambling. That might be good for Pippen's purse, but it's bad for the rest of us. It presents a bad image of Zanzibar to visitors.'

'I can't do anything to help you there, you know,' Jim said. 'Can't go around closing a legitimate business just because someone doesn't like it.' He paused. 'Unless there is some sort of town ordinance against it.'

'No,' Hazlitt said as they reached the front porch. 'That's one of the problems – there are no town ordinances at all. You know how long we've been in office, Jim. It's high on our agenda to get together with Judge O'Connell and try to draw up a city charter, but there just hasn't been the time. And, if Pippen can get all of his customers sober enough to vote one day, we won't stand a chance of passing a statute like that.'

Hazlitt was now looking worried again. He briefly rested a hand on Jim's shoulder and then confided, 'I have known Colin Pippen for a long time, Jim. He's crooked and I know it. We don't want his kind around, as we must have made clear. But if you're intent on talking to him, go ahead.

'Just one thing – the man is a habitual liar, Jim; don't take a thing he might say at face value.'

'No, there are few men I adopt that attitude toward,' Jim said, meeting Hazlitt's eyes. 'I'm on my way over to see him now, though; it has to be done. I'll stop by here on my way back.'

'I don't need to hear anything Colin Pippen has to say. I know what he'll say.'

'All right, but that's not why I was coming back here – Hazlitt, I'll need about fifty dollars to see me through.'

'Why, we've already advanced you—'

'I know what you've advanced me. I'm keeping an account. But, Mister Mayor, I have a horse to provide for. I like to eat myself. Rightfully, you should have paid my wages in advance, but since I may not be around here for long, I can understand that. But you can't just suddenly start things up on nothing more than a whim. The expenses of having a marshal, an office, and a jail go beyond just having a badge made. However long I have this job, whoever you might hire next, you people are going to have to take care of costs.'

'I suppose so,' Hazlitt said, rubbing his chin. 'As I said, I guess we just didn't think things through all the way.'

Jim wasn't sure why he said what he did next, but told Hazlitt, 'You can't buy a town on the cheap, Mister Mayor.'

Then, without expecting a response, Jim spun on his heel and made his way across the street and toward the Red Bird Saloon. Was he gaining any ground here? He couldn't say for sure. Perhaps meeting with Colin Pippen would clarify things one way or the other.

The Red Bird was relatively quiet on this morning – meaning that you had to be within a block of it to hear the hell they were raising inside. Jim knew there were plenty of men in there already from his past visits. Lonesome, solitary drinkers looking for their lives' meaning, a handful of badly hungover customers from the night before looking for some relief from their suffering, and a handful of gambling men trying to build a small stake up into a decent bit of travelling money. For no one meant to stay in Zanzibar long. This was a small-stakes town, a wide spot in the road.

Stepping down off the boardwalk where it met the alley, Jim saw a familiar figure. He was bent over at the waist as if he had a bad stomach and was trying to cure it. At Jim's call, Bernie Tibbs lifted his mournful face, wiping a hand over it.

'Oh it's you, Marshal,' the long-nosed, wide-mouthed man said. 'I'm still just a little drunk this morning – you aren't going to take me away for that, are you?'

'Where would I take you?' Jim answered. 'Although I am having a jail built. But I don't think things will get to the point where we'll be arresting men for being drunk. That would fill the jail up too fast.'

'And I suppose you'd have to feed us all,' Tibbs speculated. That was one more thing he'd have to bring up with Hazlitt and his cronies. Bernie Tibbs wiped his hand across his face and when he took it down this time, he was smiling – faintly, but smiling.

'I think I'm feeling a little better,' he told Jim. 'Out

with the bad whiskey, in with the good. That should fix me up. Don't have any money you could let me have, do you, Jim?'

'I can let you have a cartwheel if it will do you any good,' Jim Early said, fishing his lone silver dollar from his jeans. It wasn't that important to him. Hazlitt would have fifty more for him later on – if he wanted to keep his marshal in town.

'It will do me a world of good. Thanks, Jim,' Tibbs said, pocketing the dollar. 'Where are you off to this morning?'

'On my way to see Colin Pippen. It's time we had a talk.'

'Oh, you're not planning any trouble, are you Jim?'

'Furthest thing from my mind.'

'Glad to hear that,' Tibbs, who was now slowly recovering from his trembling and his pallor, said. 'Still, Jim, it's not a good idea to walk through the Red Bird just now. Around back there's a stairway leading up to the second floor where Pippen has his office.'

Jim thanked Bernie for the advice and walked that way to find the wooden steps leading up from the greasy floor of the decomposed-granite alley to the second-story office of Colin Pippen.

The man who looked up sharply at Jim's entrance was not at all what Jim had expected. He was narrow, of medium height with a hawkish face, which drooped on the left side. He wore a narrow, crooked mustache. His hair was thick, reddish brown with streaks of pure white. His eyes were dark, watery and fixed. Jim decided that he was looking at a man who had lived a hard life and was now paying the price for it. He introduced himself, which was hardly necessary with his shiny badge glinting in the lantern light.

'Ah, yes, I've been expecting you,' Pippen said in a curiously high-pitched voice that sounded unsteady to Jim. The man had suffered a stroke, Jim decided. 'Please take a chair . . . what would you like to be called? Marshal? Mr Travers? Jim Early?'

'Jim is fine.'

'All right, Jim, what can I do for you today?'

'What I'm trying to do,' Jim said, taking a seat in the offered chair, 'is to find out as much as I can about the situation in Zanzibar. I've taken this job out of necessity, but I intend to do it as well as I can and without bias.'

'Oh, I assumed you were just a hired gun with a badge,' Pippen said, He drummed on his desk with his long white fingers.

'No. Mind telling me exactly what the grudge is between you and Hazlitt and the others?'

'The problem,' Pippen said drily, 'is that I make more than the three of them combined every week, and they don't like it. The problem is that they think that the Red Bird is driving off would-be settlers who otherwise would be purchasing the empty buildings they own on Main Street, providing customers for their shops, purchasing those shoddy cottages Gerard has built in the valley, were it not for the unhealthy growth on Zanzibar's face, which is the Red Bird Saloon. Is that clear enough?'

'Sure. I already knew that. Decent folks don't want to

settle here beside the Red Bird and its rough crowd of drinking men.'

'It's so simple, Marshal, I don't know why you bothered to come up and ask me.'

'Simple in explanation, not so simple to resolve, is it?'

'I don't care to resolve it,' Colin Pippen said. His hand was now trembling, and his face had begun to twitch. 'I like things just the way they are, and giving a man a badge to talk to me is not going to sway me one inch.'

Pippen leaned forward, clasping his hands together. He glared at Jim. 'And, a man with a pistol has no chance of closing this saloon down. I have a lot of friends who also own guns.'

'I know. I've met a few of them. Do you count the Hinton brothers among them?' Jim asked.

'They're new in town, but yes, I have talked to the boys – simply because they seem familiar with you.'

'We rode a lot of hard miles together once.'

'They've told me all about it. Especially Arvin, who seems to harbor a deep grudge against you.'

'That's his problem. I've never done anything to him.'

'Except run out on them with your saddle-bags full of money, leaving both of them to be sent to prison.'

'That's not true,' Jim objected. 'Arvin can't believe that. After all, he was there.'

'Billy has no fondness for you, either. While they were locked up, you seem to have lived rich and found yourself a dance-hall princess.'

'Keep Linda Lu out of this,' Jim warned.

'All right, I will. We're both gentlemen after all.'

Were they? Jim doubted that either one of them was. He shouldn't have bothered to come to see Pippen. It was a useless exercise. He rose, putting his hat back on.

'I don't suppose you hired the Hintons or someone else to try to kill me?' Jim asked Pippen.

The man smiled crookedly. 'Why would I do that? I have no fear of you, Marshal. I have harmed no one, broken no law at all. No man in this town could ever arrest me even if I had done so – I have too many friends.'

'Let's hope it never comes to that,' Jim said. 'I'd hate to have to find out.'

'Yes.' Pippen grew momentarily thoughtful. 'I understand from Billy Hinton that you're not that good of a shot anyway.'

'Oh, that!' Jim said lightly. 'That goes back to a bet we had down in Taos. Billy wagered that I couldn't shoot off the right ear of a man called Lazlo Yates at fifty paces.'

'You missed, of course.'

'I did. I was far off the mark that morning. I shot off Lazlo's left ear.'

Jim smiled thinly and left Colin Pippen sitting behind his desk, wondering at the truth of the tale.

Jim felt more like having a drink than he had at any time in memory, but today did not seem to be the right time for it. He slipped down the outside steps and into the sun-heated, oily alley again. It was empty but for a small yellow dog.

And Arvin Hinton, who stood braced and ready, his hand dangling near the butt of his holstered Colt .44.

FIVE

Arvin Hinton was older, taller than his brother, Billy. His beard, however, had not grown in with the black flourish of Billy's. Jim supposed that men in the territorial prison found it easier to let their beards grow than to shave them. Arvin's eyes were dark and angry, glittering with malevolence.

'Well, well,' Arvin said, his fingers still twitching near his holster. 'Ain't this a surprise?'

'Not much,' Jim answered, 'I heard you were in town. Your boss told me.'

'My boss?' Arvin looked puzzled.

'Mr Pippen. Didn't he send you out to kill me?'

'I barely know Pippen,' Arvin replied. 'No one sends me to do anything. I do whatever I decide to do on my own.'

'And what have you decided to do, Arvin?'

'Get what's coming to me,' the tall man growled.

'Maybe you will,' Jim said with a hint of menace. 'But tell me – what do you think is due you?'

'My share of what you took from that bank – or have

68

you spent it all on fancy women?'

Jim ignored this latest slur on Linda Lu Finch, and with narrowed eyes told Arvin, 'You know damned well I didn't rob that bank – you were there, Arvin.'

'All I know is that you ran and left me and my brother to take the fall. What happened, Jim, did you see that deputy sheriff coming through the window?'

'No. I just suddenly lost my stomach for that particular job, seeing how much those folks over there were counting on their money being safely held for them.'

'Just suddenly went soft, huh?'

'If that's the way you want to put it.'

'The word is that you and the banker had something cooked up. He and you split the money and you send me and Billy off to the gallows.'

'That's stupid, Arvin. You say the word is out – why would you believe anything like that? You and Billy were with me the whole time!'

'You could have slipped out on us any time and set that up.'

'Arvin, I believe your brain went flat while you were locked up.'

Maybe Arvin, like so many jailed men, had just had too much time to brood and needed to blame his fate on someone else. His anger made no sense except that Jim had not been punished and he and Billy had.

'I'm not clever enough to do what you're suggesting,' Jim told his bearded, one-time friend. 'You ought to know that.'

'You're clever enough to corral yourself a fancy lady, smart enough to win twenty thousand dollars at a poker table in this poor town. You're smart enough to get yourself made marshal,' Arvin shot back, his face beginning to grow red beneath his beard.

'This business is mostly connected,' Jim said in an even voice, 'but not in the way you believe it is. Things just keep happening to me.'

'More things are going to happen,' Arvin promised.

'Don't try it, Arvin,' Jim said in warning.

'Now you're a gun hand too?' Arvin laughed. 'I've heard a few stories around town about you, but remember, we trailed together for a few years. I know how you shoot, and I know I'm better than you with a handgun.'

'Don't do it, Arvin,' Jim tried again. He knew that Arvin Hinton was acting only out of frustration and jealousy – as if anyone had a reason to be jealous of Jim Early! Knowing that did not make Arvin less dangerous. Arvin went for his pistol without another word.

Either Arvin's pistol hung up in his holster, or Jim was actually quicker than Hinton to the draw. Either way, Jim's Colt came free of leather first, and Jim fired at Arvin. His bullet caught Arvin in the left ankle, shattering it. Not the stuff gunfight legends are made of, but it was effective. Arvin's pained scream filled the alleyway and he crumpled up, flinging his pistol away as he fell.

Jim walked to the man who was writhing in pain on the ground, clutching his crushed ankle. He stood over him for a minute, shaking his head.

The sound of boot-steps approaching on the run jerked Jim's head around. He set himself, half-expecting to see Billy Hinton rushing at him, but it was Bernie

Tibbs. The thin man halted his run and approached Jim on faltering legs, looking down at Arvin sprawled on the ground.

'I thought you'd be drinking in the Red Bird,' Jim said, only now holstering his weapon.

Bernie Tibbs lifted his dark, mournful eyes and rubbed his long-whiskered jaw. 'I kinda ran out of funds, Marshal. I thought maybe I'd come looking for you.'

'If you spent that dollar already buying nickel beer, you were really drinking,' Jim said.

'Beer wasn't getting it done,' Tibbs said. 'Besides, I owed a few of the boys a couple of drinks.'

'No wonder you're broke all the time,' Jim commented. 'Listen, Bernie, how'd you like to make another five dollars? I can have it for you in almost no time.'

Bernie Tibbs' eyes opened in wonder, his narrow mouth lifted with gratitude. 'What do I have to do for it?'

'Go find a coil of rope and bring it back. Then we're going to tie up this man.' He tilted his head toward Arvin, who had stopped writhing but lay with his eyes rolled back, still gripping his broken ankle. 'You'll have to stand guard over him somewhere after we take him prisoner.'

'You mean I'm sort of a temporary deputy?' Tibbs asked. His expression was not appreciative. The men of Zanzibar did not view the law in a kindly way.

'That's what you are, for the time being – if you want to make five dollars,' Jim said. 'I can always find someone else, I suppose—'

'Don't do that, Marshal!' Tibbs said with a drunkard's greed. 'I'll take the job. I'm off now to find some rope.'

Tibbs went off, running as best he could on spindly, half-sober legs.

'I need a doctor,' Arvin moaned.

'Sure. Any idea of where to find one?' A doctor was one more thing Zanzibar lacked.

'You're not going to help me?' Arvin asked with angry disbelief.

'But I am,' Jim Early said. 'I'm only going to tie you up, not use the rope to hang you.'

'Billy will take care of you,' Arvin threatened.

'Maybe, maybe not. You two might just find yourselves cellmates again. What's the matter, Arvin, couldn't you take the freedom you had?'

'I just. . . .' Arvin started mumbling, babbling on about old complaints again, and Jim quit listening as he waited for Tibbs to get back. It would have been a good time to have a jail available.

Bound tightly, Arvin was lifted to his feet ten minutes later. His eyes flickered between pure hate and a plea for pity. 'Let's go, Arvin.'

'You want me to walk, Jim? Why, you know I can't! Can't you get a wagon or something?'

'No I can't, Arvin. It's not in the budget. Next time get yourself shot in a more civilized town.'

'Why, you bastard!' Arvin screamed as they hoisted him to his feet. He followed with a series of well-pronounced obscenities as they forced him to hobble, hop, and drag his way along the alley.

'Count yourself lucky, Arvin,' Jim Early said. 'I could just as easily have hit you in the heart or shot your brain through your eye.' Which was a groundless boast since Jim knew better than anyone else that beating Arvin to the draw and managing to hit him at all was a matter of chance. But, he had always clung to the concept that the more his reputation was burnished, the smaller the chance of someone with a gun challenging him.

Jim had scooped up Arvin's pistol and plunked the convict's hat back on his head before they left the alley, and just before staggering off, had seen the crooked man standing on the top landing of the outer staircase, watching them with curiosity. If this had all been Colin Pippen's idea, his first attempt on Jim Early's life had failed before his eyes.

'I'm getting tired of toting this man,' Jim said. 'What's that over there?'

'In the middle of the street?' Bernie Tibbs asked. 'Why, that's the flagpole we put up last year on the Fourth of July.'

'That'll do,' Jim said. 'Take him over there.'

Arvin was taken to the fifty-foot-tall barked-pine pole, which stood in the middle of the dusty street, and was tied to it. 'Here,' Jim said, handing Arvin's pistol to Tibbs. 'Shoot him if he tries anything, though I can't see him running off even if he could get free.'

'Jim, please!' Arvin wailed. Now he was to be subjected to sitting on public display, tied to a pole for gawkers and gibers to see. 'Listen to me!'

'No, Arvin,' Jim answered. 'I tried to talk things out

with you and all I got for my efforts was you drawing down on me. We have nothing more to say to each other.'

The result of Jim Early's first arrest was not the most desirable, but it would serve a dual purpose. First of all people would know that Jim had bested Arvin Hinton and he meant to go about his work seriously. Secondly, the sight of the town's first prisoner being tied like a dog in the heat and dust of the day for all to see might prod Mayor Hazlitt and the other members of the town council to expedite the building of a jail.

'Marshal?' Bernie Tibbs' face was again sorrowful. 'I suppose I don't mind watching this man for you, though I'll hear some comments in the Red Bird later, but ... do you think you'll be coming back soon?'

'Yes, I will. What's the matter, Bernie?'

'It's nothing – well, yes, it is! I don't want to start getting the trembles this early. If a man only had a small bottle of liquor for comfort, this wouldn't be such a bad form of work.'

'I can do that for you,' Jim promised. And if the mayor and town council didn't like it, they could fire both Jim and Bernie Tibbs.

Mayor Hazlitt was standing with Peter Wiley in front of Wiley's Main Street store when Jim approached them. Hazlitt's pointing finger was trembling.

'What in the hell is that supposed to be?' he demanded.

The flagpole where Arvin Hinton sat tethered was no more than two hundred feet from the store. Jim tipped back his hat and told the two businessmen, 'Oh, that's

Arvin Hinton. I had to arrest him; he came after me with a gun.'

'You just can't tie a man up in the middle of the street and leave him,' Hazlitt said. He looked nearly apoplectic. His face was beet-red. 'What if we had visiting men interested in setting up shop in Zanzibar, and the first thing they saw was a man tied to the town flagpole?' Hazlitt's voice sputtered away to indignant silence.

'It's not a welcoming sight,' Jim agreed. 'But what else am I supposed to do with a man who's threatening the local peace officer with a gun? As soon as you men get the jail constructed, I'll move him over there. But in the meantime he is a caution to other men not to break the law.'

Jim paused, smiled, and said to Hazlitt, 'If you don't have that fifty dollars for me yet, can you advance me five? I have to pay the deputy who's watching Hinton.'

'Deputy?' Peter Wiley exclaimed. 'Why, that's Bernie Tibbs, a no-account drunk!'

'Yes, sir, it is. At the time I needed some help, and men weren't exactly clamoring for the job.'

'Did you shoot Hinton?' Hazlitt asked dolefully.

'Yes, sir, I did. He asked for it.'

'This is not the way things were supposed to go,' Wiley said. He was more miserable than Hazlitt, judging by his expression.

'It's the way they have gone,' Jim Early said. 'Let's just take care of the problems at hand as they come along, shall we? First, I need five bucks for Bernie Tibbs or he won't remain out there for long. Second, I need that fifty for office expenses. Third, so that we don't have a recurrence of this, I need that office and jail as soon as it can possibly be done.'

'Seems to me that you're getting kind of pushy, Marshal,' Hazlitt said.

'Does it? I understand that you men have other priorities – your businesses – and I am only a part of your interests. Let me have enough money, the resources I need to ease this area of concern for you, then you can get back to what you do best.'

'Dammit, Peter,' Hazlitt said, 'the man's right. All right, Jim, do what you have to do. Frank Gerard will let us have the old confectionery across the street for your office. There's a storeroom that can probably be converted to a jail. I'll send Kesselring over to take a look. For the time being,' he grumbled a little more and dug into his pocket, pulling a handful of coins from it, 'here's the fifty dollars – do what you can with it, but don't come back for more any time soon.'

'I'll try not to,' Jim said, pocketing the money. 'Have you talked to Judge O'Connell to find out if we have any statutes or ordinances in this town?'

'There hasn't been time,' Hazlitt said, trying for a soothing voice. 'It's still early in the day. We'll meet with him as soon as possible. We should be able to enact some sort of emergency measures today.'

'Do your best,' Jim said with a nod, 'that's what I'm going to do. Let me know when I can move into the office. Kesselring won't bother me working around me.'

'Sometime today,' Hazlitt said. 'It won't be completed

for a while, you understand.'

'I'll trust to the smith to do his best,' Jim replied. 'As long as there's a chair in there, I'll make out. And – you haven't forgotten about hanging a shingle outside, have you? I want everyone to be able to find me.'

The mayor and Wiley watched as Jim returned to the flagpole and slipped Bernie Tibbs a five-dollar gold piece.

'Peter,' Hazlitt said, 'I hope for our sakes that the man knows what he's doing.'

'I hope for his sake that he does,' Wiley said before turning and re-entering his emporium, where customers were waiting. He was worried about many small points. To top it off he had not seen Frank Gerard all day. Where was he? This whole proposition had been his idea in the first place, after all.

No matter – Wiley got back to work, losing himself in the job of trying to satisfy his customers.

Striding once more along the street toward the empty lot where Ben Lytle had chosen to die, Jim took his time in going into each shop along the way. He wore his badge prominently displayed now, hoping to nudge a little more cooperation from the citizens of Zanzibar. After completing his interviews, frustration building, he returned to the stable to fetch his gray horse.

He did not now have the feeling that anyone was withholding information from him; it seemed only that there was no one who had actually seen the events of that morning.

Arvin Hinton was dozing uncomfortably in the sun and

dust of Main Street. He managed to open one eye and give Jim an evil glance as he passed by on his horse. Bernie Tibbs, who was perched on a bucket he had gotten from somewhere, lifted a hand to Jim Early. The thin man didn't appear completely drunk. He was holding Arvin's pistol loosely in one hand, a pint whiskey bottle in the other.

Where was Billy Hinton? The bearded man would know that attempting a rescue of his brother in the middle of the street in broad daylight was extremely hazardous, but he might also believe that with only a half-drunk Bernie Tibbs standing guard – a man who was unlikely to shoot back – it was the best chance he would have. Billy could not know what Jim's plans for Arvin were. If Billy was as filled with bad information as his brother, he might believe that Jim would hang his brother. Jim had made no determination yet on what to do with Arvin. That would have to be up to the judge, which reminded Jim again that he had to find the opportunity to meet with O'Connell, whom he had not so much as seen yet.

No one else in this town seemed to have a real idea what plans, procedures, laws they meant to implement in Zanzibar. That left it up to Jim. He paused mentally – long enough to wonder whether he cared about Zanzibar and their plans at all. He was looking for his stolen money, enough to move on with Linda Lu, nothing more. To move on to some larger town where Linda would be happier, perhaps more loving, as she had been when he had first plucked her from her past circumstances and blithely promised her the world.

The door to the confectionery shop that was to be his office stood open, Jim saw. A crudely painted sign reading 'Marshal's Office' hung from the awning. He decided he might as well have a look inside. Directly across the street stood Hazlitt's feed and grain store, but there was no sign of the mayor, for which Jim was grateful. He had had his fill of politics for the day.

Two sawhorses stood on the front porch of the shop, their feet deep in sawdust. Inside the shop a hammer cracked three times and a metal fixture creaked. Jim slipped inside to see a bulky man with a clean-shaven face hefting a heavy door as he tried to position it in a rebuilt doorway. This must be Jan Kesselring.

'Need a hand?' Jim asked.

Kesselring turned his head and nodded. 'Need another inch to get the eye of this hinge on to the pin.'

'Let's see if I can help,' Jim said. He stepped forward. Not a small man, Jim felt dwarfed by the blacksmith, whose arms were nearly the size of Jim's thighs.

'Use that pry bar there,' Kesselring said. 'I have to guide this up.' Jim did as he was told and the door rose just enough to settle on to the heavy iron hinges.

'You the marshal?' Kesselring asked, stepping back to mop at his brow.

'That's right.'

'What I decided to do, since this was described to me as a hurry-up job, was to use this old arched oak door I've had around for a while. The planks are four inches thick. I think it must have come from some old Spanish church. I dunno. I kept it around in case I had a use for it someday.

'I had to cut it down a little. It fits all right now. What I mean to do next is cut a square in it about head high and install some bars. I'll pin them to iron plate on either side of the door. No one's going to break out of there, Marshal, I'll guarantee that. Tomorrow I'll be back with some planks and chains and I'll hang two beds from the walls.'

'Sounds good to me,' Jim said. 'I think you've done a great job considering how much time you've had to plan things out.'

'One day we'll fashion a right iron cell – working metal is my craft. When the town council – is that what they're calling themselves? – comes up with the money to buy stock with, that is.'

'Keep it in mind,' Jim said. 'One day you might be called on again.'

'Well,' Kesselring was still mopping his brow, 'I done my best given the circumstances.' The big man grinned. 'They said that the marshal wanted the job done right now!'

'It'll do,' Jim replied. Looking around the small office he saw that two wooden chairs had been brought in. They now stood stacked in the corner atop a chipped, slightly lopsided desk.

'Yeah,' Kesselring said, seeing the direction of Jim Early's gaze. 'Those were left from the confectionery shop. I found them in the storeroom. I remember that desk from a long time back. I'll straighten it up a little before I leave.'

'I'd appreciate it, Jan. You're a good man.'

'I only do my best with every job I get and hope they keep coming,' Kesselring said. 'By the way, Marshal – there's an envelope some woman brought in for you about an hour ago. On the desk.'

'A woman? 'What woman?' Jim asked, walking toward the stack of furniture.

'I was too busy to see,' Kesselring said, 'I just heard her voice from inside the cell.'

'Young? Old?' Jim asked, finding the yellow envelope.

'I couldn't tell,' the blacksmith said. 'Not from her voice.'

Jim shrugged mentally and opened the unsealed envelope to find a small sheet of folded paper inside. There was only one sentence written there:

Dandy Trout has your money.

SIX

Jim read the short note three times. Kesselring was gathering a few tools, preparing to leave the shop.

'Jan? Who is Dandy Trout?'

'I don't know, Marshal.' The big man scratched his head. 'It seems like a name I've heard before, but I don't rightly know who he is.'

Jim pulled one of the chairs from the stack and sat down at it, staring again at the note, written in a woman's hand. Who was Dandy Trout? And who was the woman who had brought the note, and how did she know that this Dandy Trout had Jim's poker winnings?

Well, someone in town would know the man.

Jim sat for a few minutes more, watching as Kesselring straightened the sagging desk with a block of wood and a few deft hammer strokes. Straightening up, the big man nodded and asked, 'Well, Marshal, that's it, where are you going to set up shop?'

Jim waved a hand around the empty room. 'Just shove it over in front of me, I guess.' When Kesselring had tugged and nudged the desk around, Jim put the flat of his hands on the top of it, blew off a small collection of sawdust and announced, 'I guess that's it, Jan. This place is now open for business.'

Jan provided Jim with a heavy lock and two brass keys that fitted to secure it to the barrel hasp on the door, promised to be back in the morning to install the bars in the window he had cut into the door, and went out.

Jim sat in the silence, looking around the empty marshal's office – he would have to start calling it that – and wondered, now what? He could go down the street and bring in his only prisoner, Arvin Hinton, but then he would need someone to watch the man. Maybe Bernie Tibbs wouldn't mind doing that for a few hours. He would be out of the sun, have a chair to sit on – the other could be given to Arvin as a temporary perch before Kesselring returned to install the bunks in the cell.

Arvin would be safely locked away – as a precaution, Jim did not intend to leave the keys in Bernie's possession. Maybe the little man wouldn't mind sweeping out the mess left by Kesselring and cleaning off the front porch. Bernie was well stocked with whiskey for the time being, and he could quit any time he liked. That would leave Jim free to pursue his work, which consisted of finding his stolen money, and the strongest clue he had as to what had happened to it would seem to be this man Dandy Trout.

An hour later with these arrangements made, Jim started homeward once again, leaving a wobbly, weaving Bernie Tibbs to supervise Arvin Hinton, who seemed almost comatose after being wounded and spending a day in the sun. Maybe someone knew of a man with some medical experience who could do something for the injured convict. Not that Jim felt any pity for the man who had tried to kill him, but even a dog deserves some help when it's injured.

First things first, Jim decided as he stepped into the saddle of his gray horse. He needed to find out how Linda Lu was coping with the situation. He could not have her running off on to the desert without a dollar in her purse and no idea where she might be headed, and he knew she was capable of it. Headstrong was too mild a word for Linda Lu Finch.

He would just ask her to be patient a little longer, tell her that he now had an idea where his money had gone – even if it was only that, an idea.

After a not unpleasant ride through the warmth of the day, he found the sandy path where cottonwoods flourished, leading to the cottages. As he neared the house he saw that there was a freight wagon parked in front of it. Frowning, he turned his horse's head that way.

Now what?

Jim swung down and tied his horse to the hitch rail as two bulky men emerged into the heat of the day, wiping at their brows and grumbling between themselves. Jim heard one of them say, 'I've had more particular customers, but I can't remember when.'

After a glance at Jim, the men clambered to the bench seat of the wagon, turned their team, and headed back toward town. He heard another word muttered . . . 'marshal', in a disparaging tone.

Jim tramped into the cottage, removing his hat. He recognized only the plush yellow chair in the living room. The emptiness of the rest of the room had been filled with new furniture; the upholstered items in pale blue, the tables of polished mahogany. Linda Lu, looking quite pleased with herself, swept into the room. She wore her dark-blue dress with the black lace at the cuffs and throat.

'Hello, Jim. What do you think?'

'I don't know what to think. It looks very nice, but where did you get it all?'

'Frank sent it over.'

'Frank who?'

'Frank Gerard, of course,' Linda said, eyeing Jim as if he were a slow student. 'It's all from the Strawberry Heights Hotel. He is the hotel's owner, you know. There are a lot of unused rooms there, and Frank generously offered us the use of some of the furniture. There are dishes and glasses, utensils in the kitchen from the hotel restaurant. You should see our bed,' Linda told him, taking his hand and tugging him that way.

Jim recognized the bed. This one or one like it was the one he and Linda had shared at the hotel. It was neatly made with an off-orange coverlet thrown over it.

'Well?' Linda asked brightly. She was happier, that was for sure.

'It's got to beat sleeping on the floor,' was Jim's answer. But he wondered, 'Why did Gerard do this for us?' The man with the flowing red mustache had not struck Jim as the soul of generosity.

'Well, you do work for him, Jim. For the town.

Weren't you provided with an office as well?'

'Yes, I was,' Jim said, looking down into Linda's sparkling eyes.

She shrugged. 'That was Frank's doing too. He said he couldn't expect the town marshal to sleep in the open and have no place to conduct his work.'

'Not when he was traveling with a beautiful woman,' Jim muttered.

'What was that?' Linda asked. 'Well, of course Frank was concerned about me, too. We've become quite good friends in a short time. I knew some good was bound to come out of you taking that job.' She turned from him to part the sheer curtains on the bedroom window. Pausing in her movements abruptly, she said, 'I almost forgot to tell you. A man named Kyle Colson was asking about you at the restaurant. I was pointed out to him and he came over to my table. He said to tell you that he was looking forward to seeing you. Do you know who he is?'

'We've never met,' Jim said. But, yes, he did know who Colson was. He was a well-known West Texas gunfighter. Colson was reputed to have killed at least twenty men. What could a man like that want with Jim? Unless he had been sent for. Jim wondered if he could be someone the Hinton brothers had met in prison, told about the supposed bank funds he had stolen.

He also wondered about Colin Pippen; was it possible that the owner of the Red Bird had decided to hire a gun hand in case the Zanzibar town council did decide to try to uproot him? There was no telling. Jim could only keep his eyes open for the man, although he did not know what Colson looked like, nor even have a description of him. Maybe someone would know. More important to Jim on this day was finding the mysterious Dandy Trout, who had been identified by an unknown woman as the possessor of the green bag filled with Jim's poker-table winnings.

With the recovery of that money he and Linda Lu could head out for anywhere – Santa Fe, perhaps – and be done with all of Zanzibar's politics and puzzles.

Bothering Jim on a more personal level was Frank Gerard. He did not like the man hanging around Linda. He knew that Linda could handle Gerard – she had been fending off such men's intentions most of her life – but still, Jim didn't have to like it.

She was hardly a naïve woman; she must have known what was behind Gerard's recent attention, but she was enough of an actress to enjoy the attention while offering false promises to her would-be suitors. That was the way she had been in Las Cruces and probably always would be.

Jim continued to poke around the house and the kitchen, taking a quick inventory of what they had. In another minute Linda bustled out, wearing a flimsy black shawl over her shoulders. Her lips had been newly painted.

'You act like you're going somewhere,' Jim said, leaning against the kitchen door jamb.

'I am. Frank asked me to lunch at the hotel. I could hardly refuse after all he's done for us.'

'No,' Jim said woodenly, 'you could hardly refuse.'

'Jim!' Linda scolded, rising on tiptoes to kiss him

lightly. 'Surely you can't be unhappy with me for trying to make a few friends in town. You're the one who told me we should try rubbing elbows with the town's leading citizens.'

'Did I?' Jim asked unhappily.

'You certainly did!' Linda said. 'So you see, I do pay attention to what you say . . . sometimes.'

Then with one of her irresistible smiles she pulled her shawl up tighter and started toward the open door of the cottage. She stopped and turned back.

'After all, Jim, you have your own new friends as well. I need some sort of company.'

Yes, he had made friends in Zanzibar. The Hinton brothers. Colin Pippen. Bernie Tibbs. Kyle Colson. He didn't think any of them was likely to invite him to lunch at the hotel.

'I didn't get the chance to look through the cupboards, Linda,' he called as she went through the doorway. 'Did Frank Gerard bring a can of beans for me?'

No, not that, nor anything else, he discovered as Linda drove her buggy away and he prowled the cabinets. He was glad that Linda, at least, was having a good time, he thought sourly. Then he realized that that was all he had wanted for her in the first place and mentally scolded himself for his pettiness. After all, he knew how to feed himself.

Riding back into town he spotted Linda's buggy outside the Strawberry Heights Hotel. In a sulky mood he continued on to Ethel M's restaurant. As he swung down at the hitch rail he could smell corned beef and cabbage cooking. Well, that sounded good to him just then. He wondered vaguely if Ginnie Cummings was working there today. And what was this trouble she had hinted at? The girl had a cheerful smile, at least, and Jim thought he could use one just then. Of course, Jim knew that with some waitresses that smile only lasted until they put their pads down and went off work. No matter, Jim would accept even a meaningless, professional smile on this hot, dusty day. It would brighten his own mood for a little while.

On his way in the front plank door of the restaurant he glanced up and down the street, not really expecting to see anyone he was looking for. After all, the two men he was watching out for – Kyle Colson and Dandy Trout – were both unknown faces to him. After he ate he would have to return to the jail, perhaps taking some food along for Bernie Tibbs. He dared not take the man another bottle of liquor. Tibbs had been in Zanzibar for a long while. He might know who this Dandy Trout was. He might also ask the man about Kyle Colson, though it was unlikely that Tibbs had run across the Texas gunman in his limited travels.

Afterward, Jim decided, closing the white-painted door behind him as he entered the restaurant, he had to make the time to find Judge O'Connell and talk to him. He needed to have some idea of what laws he was supposed to enforce. Outside of high crimes, which were covered by territorial law, he was at a loss as to what activities were banned, prohibited in Zanzibar. There were no town ordinances, no local bans so far as he knew. His was not a job that should be done in the dark.

Ginnie was waiting tables, but the restaurant was bustling just then. It seemed unlikely that they would have the time to talk. Jim found himself seated at a small table in the back corner of the room. When Ginnie approached him, she was juggling a tray with stacks of dishes on it.

'I see you've got an office now,' she said, blowing a strand of blonde hair off her cheek as she waited for Jim's order.

He said, 'Yes. Just come over any time – although I haven't spent much time there yet.'

Someone called to Ginnie from across the crowded room and Jim told her, 'Just let me have the corned beef and cabbage – and a couple of corned beef sandwiches to go, if you can.'

She started to say something and then hurried away. Jim understood that; the place was busy. He never knew how these women could handle a crowded restaurant as well as they did. It was all push and shove with a constant clamor and demands being shouted out. Ginnie deserved better. But there was nothing better, he supposed. Not in Zanzibar.

Jim ate without enjoying the food much. He watched Ginnie, feeling sorry for the haggard young woman. Long hours, low pay. Not many men in Zanzibar understood the idea of tipping for service. Few, indeed, that patronized Ethel M's. He wished he could do something to help her. . . .

Jim yanked his thoughts up short. That was exactly the kind of thinking that had led him to adopt Linda Lu down in Las Cruces. Jim Early scolded himself for still not learning that he hadn't the resources a shining knight needed.

Ginnie made her way back to his table with a brown paper bag. 'Two sandwiches,' she told him as she totaled the bill. Jim smiled; he had seen the cuffs of her blue jeans poking out from beneath her black skirt again. As soon as the lunch rush was over Ginnie would be out back, scraping dishes again.

The crowd was thinning rapidly, so Jim asked her, 'Do you know a man named Dandy Trout, Ginnie?'

'Dandy Trout. Sure I know him. He's a harmless little fellow who lives in a shack out on Bedel Road. Do you know where that is?'

'I'll find it. Thank you, Ginnie,' Jim said, rising. He gave her the cost of the meal and when she turned away placed another silver dollar on the table near his plate.

Outside the sun was still high, beaming down through a cloudless sky. It was warm, dusty – as it had been every day since his arrival in Zanzibar. A kid with flapping soles on his shoes was running past and Jim held him up long enough to ask, 'Can you tell me where Bedel Road is?'

'Well, sure,' the boy said, eyeing Jim Early as if he were the dumbest man he had ever met. Jim tossed the kid a nickel of the town's money and started on his way out of town, following the directions he had been given. The land was yellow and dry. A few scattered live oak trees stood among the wild oats and patches of brown grama grass. Some purple mustard, which seemed to flourish in the heat, grew here and there. A flock of jittery crows rose from the trees, scolding and

91

wheeling in the air.

Jim rode warily ahead. He did not know Dandy Trout, and did not know that he was a harmless little fellow as Ginnie had told him. Dandy might have been involved with Ben Lytle in robbing him – some unknown woman had thought so – and that alone was enough to make Dandy Trout dangerous. If he had Jim's money, Trout was unlikely to simply shrug and hand it over.

Ahead now Jim could make out a flat, shallow pond with dried mud at its fringes. It had not rained for a while and the pond was shrinking in the heat. To the west, his right, Jim saw a little patchwork cabin sitting back in the shade of a cottonwood grove. Dark, dumpy, and leaning, the shack looked like someplace deserted, but it seemed to be Dandy Trout's home.

Jim reined in the gray among the sun-silvered cottonwoods and listened. He heard nothing but the breeze playing through the leaves of the trees, the still-raucous crows. He walked his horse forward, with his Winchester rifle now unsheathed. Jim's eyes were narrowed, his jaw set. This was as close as he had gotten to his stolen money and he meant to have it back. Everything depended on recovering that money.

Nothing stirred around the ramshackle cabin. The day held silent and hot. All right, then, he would just have to approach the shack and knock on the door. He glanced once at the shallow pond where the sun reflected off its face like a mirror and went on.

The gray horse balked, lifted its head, and snorted, taking a few steps back. Jim's frown deepened. The gray was a stolid animal, not given to antics. The only time the horse had acted that way in the past was when it had encountered a rattlesnake along the trail.

Jim scanned the ground ahead of them. He saw nothing of a snake.

But a little man in his ragged clothes lay still in the shadows cast by the trees.

SEVEN

The harmless little man was dead. Jim had to assume that he was Dandy Trout. How many harmless little men could there be lying around the shack? Dandy was definitely harmless now, that was certain. Crouching, Jim examined the body, keeping his eyes moving around the area, for Trout had been murdered. Shot at close range at the base of his skull and left for dead. Jim sat back on his heels and took a deep breath. There was nothing like the green bag Ben Lytle had used for his robbery in sight. Nor would there be. Men don't execute a harmless soul for no reason and then leave a bagful of money lying around. Jim felt obliged to search the shack, although whoever had committed this crime would have already done so if he needed to, leaving nothing behind.

He entered through the door, which was badly hung on leather hinges, and poked around, finding what he had expected: nothing worthwhile. There was a bed with a straw-stuffed mattress, a few plank shelves holding chipped cups and dishes, a rickety puncheon chair – and nothing else. He searched around for hiding places, loose planks, hidden nooks, but he found none and there was little space in the tiny cabin that could be used for concealment.

Disappointed, angry, Jim returned to his horse. He had come too late. He should have ridden out as soon as he got the accusing note the woman had left. No matter now; it was done and he was back to being a pauper.

Jim wondered what a real marshal would have done with the body. Send some people in town out to bury it, he supposed. Instead he hefted the man, who seemed to weigh little in death, over the reluctant gray's withers and started back toward Zanzibar.

Emerging from the shadows beneath the trees, Jim squinted into the brilliant sunlight. He had ridden only a hundred feet or so before the concealed rifleman fired at him. The shot was a miss, slamming into the unhappy Dandy Trout's body with a heavy slapping sound.

Jim grabbed for his rifle and kicked free of the stirrups, rolling to the ground. The gray horse, confused and frightened, danced away. Dandy Trout's head bobbed wildly, his arms and legs flapping before he slipped from the horse to lie like a human puddle in the yellow grass.

Jim rolled to one side and took up a prone position concealed only by the thin screen of golden wild oats on the valley floor. Nothing moved. The wind had whipped away the gunsmoke, leaving no target.

The white sun coasted through the pale-blue sky. Jim

wiped the sweat from his eyes. His hands were slick with perspiration on his Winchester. He dared not move. There were many oak trees on the knoll opposite him, offering concealment for the sniper. He saw no shadow, no bit of color, no glint of sunlight on metal. He could only wait and watch as the damnable crows continued to wheel and caw overhead.

Jim's horse, he saw thankfully, had not wandered far. It stood, head down, tugging at some dry grass. The unfortunate Trout lay sprawled against the hot earth, having suffered the final indignity.

Jim wondered if the rifleman, distant as he was, could have mistaken Trout's body for his and counted the job done. It seemed unlikely, but it could have been so. After all, a man usually rides alone, not carrying a spare corpse. At a distance, with the sun in his eyes his ambusher might have ... Jim's thoughts broke off, diverted by the ticklish feel on his left hand. A scorpion had made its way there, and Jim flicked the nasty little beast away.

Still there was no visible movement in the trees across the meadow. The ambusher could have simply tired of waiting and slipped away. Or, he could still, with extraordinary patience, be waiting for Jim Early to move and give him a clear shot.

Who was it that had done the shooting? Jim pondered that for a while. Billy Hinton was certainly capable of it. There was also the hired gunman, Kyle Colson, to consider. But Colson was a short-gun man and his style would have been more to meet Jim in some dark alley. But that was supposition. Who else?

There was Colin Pippen, of course, but Jim couldn't conceive of the saloon owner riding out here on his own to bushwhack him. Besides, Pippen had shown no obvious fear of Jim Early or the machinations of the town council. If he had actually hired Colson's gun, he would let the gunfighter take care of things for him.

He had no good guess, and it didn't matter. What mattered now was getting out of there alive and making his way back to Zanzibar. With his eyes fixed on the far oaks, Jim moved tentatively, shifting his position a few feet to the left. Enough to make himself briefly visible, but not enough for a clear shot. His movement brought no fire from the knoll.

The day was shortening, but there was no hint of sunset in the long skies. Jim was hot, thirsty, cramped with inaction. He swatted at a cluster of gnats that had drifted before his face. From where he now lay, he could see a gathering of bluebottle flies on Dandy Trout's waxen face. It was a disturbing sight, perhaps carrying a foreboding of Jim's own death.

He had to move. Let the sniper, if he was still positioned on the knoll, take his best shot!

Jim thought he could whistle up the gray and swing aboard quickly. Somehow he felt obligated not to abandon Dandy Trout. He shook his head at his own vagaries. He had owed nothing to Trout in life; why, then, should he feel that the little man was owed that much in death?

He let out a low whistle and the gray lifted its head from its grazing and walked toward him, shying as it

97

passed Trout's body. With the horse in front of him, Jim popped up and placed his rifle across the saddle bow, ready to respond to any shots. There were none.

There was nothing at all; the day remained silent except for the damnable crows circling overhead. With a deal of effort Jim managed to position the horse, hoist Trout's body and replace it over the animal's neck, his eyes constantly on the knoll. Then he swung aboard and hurried the horse toward Zanzibar.

Jim entered the town by a circular route, pulling up behind his marshal's office, which he noticed had the back door standing open. Frowning, he swung down. Bernie would have to be told about that … unless someone had already been inside, releasing Arvin Hinton and silencing his deputy.

But everything was as it should have been inside the office. Well, everything was pretty much as he had expected. A glance into the cell showed Arvin Hinton lying on his side against the floor, his legs drawn up. Arvin did not look up. Bernie Tibbs sat behind the marshal's desk, his feet on it. He was slack-jawed, smiling to himself in some whiskey dream. Jim determined that he would have to find someone more reliable. How he was to tell the town council that he needed a paid deputy, if such a man could be found, was something he'd have to figure out later.

Jim shook Bernie's shoulder and the drunken man grumbled, stirred, and slowly opened his bloodshot eyes. 'Oh, howdy, Marshal,' Tibbs said, stretching his scrawny arms overhead.

'Howdy yourself,' Jim said grumpily, sitting on a

corner of the desk. 'Listen, Bernie, you left the back door to this place open. You know what could have happened to you, don't you?'

'Yeah, I do,' Bernie said. 'I only meant to leave it open for a while – for the air. I dozed off and forgot to close it.'

'Keep it locked,' Jim instructed the man strongly. A better idea would be to have Jan Kesselring block the door off permanently. A confectionery store might have needed it; a jail did not.

'Listen, Bernie,' Jim said, shaking the man's shoulder once more. Tibbs seemed ready to pass out again. 'What do people in Zanzibar usually do with a dead man?'

'Why, we generally bury them, Marshal,' Tibbs said around a yawn.

'Yes. Who usually does the honors is what I'm asking.'

'You know Matt over at the Joker Stable? Him and his brother, Andy, usually take care of such things.'

'Well, have someone call him over here,' Jim said. 'I've an unlively man outside.'

'You killed someone, Marshal!' Bernie looked surprised and somehow disappointed in Jim.

'No, I didn't. But he's dead. A man named Dandy Trout. Did you know him, Bernie?'

'Little old Dandy? Sure I knew him. Nicest little fellow you'd ever want to meet.'

'Well, take a peek at him, would you? I was told it's Dandy Trout, but I've never even seen the man before today.'

'Sure thing, sure thing,' Bernie said. He paused for a moment to look hopefully at the empty whiskey bottle on the desk.

'You might as well swing by the Red Bird and get another,' Jim said. He was resigned to his deputy's ways. Another man would have to be found somewhere, but for now Bernie Tibbs was the only available help.

'Thanks, Marshal,' Tibbs said with a loose smile. 'You know, this ain't such bad work.' Getting to his feet, Bernie hesitated and asked, 'Do you know Ben Lovesy, Marshal?'

'Can't say that I've ever heard the name,' Jim replied, taking a seat in the vacated marshal's chair.

'He's a good man,' Tibbs said. 'An older fellow. During the war he was a surgeon's assistant. Ben says most of what he did was holding down a soldier's arm or leg so that the doctor could saw it off. What I was thinking, though, is that we have to try to do something about the prisoner.' He lifted his chin toward the cell. 'And Ben Lovesy is about the only man in Zanzibar with any sort of medical experience. It might be an idea to bring him over before the night settles in – Ben does most of his drinking in the late hours.'

'Having sentimental feelings for our poor wounded prisoner, are you?'

'Hardly. But, Marshal when he comes around, the man can moan and scream loud enough to make your skin crawl.'

'Makes it hard to sleep, does he?'

Tibbs smiled again. 'There's that, too. But we should do something for the man if we can, shouldn't we?'

'Yes,' Jim agreed, feeling less compassion for Arvin Hinton than he should have. It's hard to raise caring impulses for a man who has tried to kill you. 'All right,' he agreed. 'If you find this Ben Lovesy at the Red Bird, have him come over. There's a few dollars in it for him. Tell him to bring any sort of medical supplies he may have.

'First,' Jim reminded his deputy, 'look at the dead man and make sure it is Dandy Trout. And send Matt or his brother over to see about burying him.'

'I got you,' Bernie said, planting his hat. 'Send Matt or Andy over. Talk to Ben Lovesy.'

'And keep your visit to the Red Bird short,' Jim said.

'I'll just bring the bottle home,' Bernie said. 'You want me on duty again, right?'

If it could be called that, Jim thought, but he was in no mood to split hairs. He still had things to do that afternoon, and high on his list was talking to Judge O'Connell before office hours had ended. He followed Bernie to the back door, threw the bolt after he had passed through, and returned to the desk. Should he start keeping a record of how his time was spent? He decided not to until someone else brought it up. He was, however, going to keep track of expenditures. His fifty dollars, seeming large enough to manage things temporarily, was rapidly shrinking. Hiring Matt and Andy to bury Dandy Trout, and Ben Lovesy to try to patch Arvin up, was going to deplete his funds even more.

Mayor Hazlitt and the other council members would balk at paying the price to have law established in

Zanzibar, but they were the ones who had initiated the plan. A knock at the front door brought Jim's head around. Walking that way he opened up to find Jan Kesselring standing there, toolbox and iron stock in hand. A few heavy planks were leaning against the outside wall of the jail.

'Come to put those bars in the cell-door window, and hang the bunks from the wall,' Jan said. Noticing Jim's uncertain look he asked, 'Is this a bad time?'

'No. No it's not; the sooner everything is done, the better. We've got a prisoner in the cell now; can you work with him there?'

'Is he armed?' the blacksmith asked.

'Of course not.'

'Then he won't bother me,' Kesselring said, and the huge smith grinned.

'How long will you be?' Jim asked, leading Kesselring across the room to the cell, the brass key in his hand.

'Not long. Less than an hour, I'd say.'

'All right. It's just that I have places to be, and my deputy isn't back yet.'

'Your deputy? Oh, you mean Bernie Tibbs. He's still drinking off your nickel, is he?'

'Yes,' Jim had to admit. 'But I haven't got anybody else just now.'

Kesselring dropped his iron stock to the floor, bringing a moan of complaint from Arvin inside the cell.

'You know,' Kesselring said, 'I've a cousin who's looking for work just now. He was working as a teamster, but the freight line went bust. Things aren't exactly booming around Zanzibar.'

'Trustworthy man, is he?'

'The most trustworthy – a good man. His name's Warren, Warren Dodge. A sober, God-fearing man.'

'I wonder if he would like this kind of work,' Jim mused. 'It doesn't suit everyone. Tell me, Jan, is he younger or older than you? Is he built along your lines?'

'Warren is twenty-five years old, Marshal. I used to tease him for fun, until he got his growth. He's a more sizeable man than I am now.'

Jim studied Kesselring with disbelief. There was someone around larger than the huge blacksmith? Not that size was that important to Jim, but it didn't hurt to have an intimidating presence in the law business. It saved a few scuffles that a lesser man might have to put up with.

'You have him come and talk to me,' Jim said and Kesselring said that he would do that.

Jim unlocked Arvin's cell so that the blacksmith could place the iron bars in the door's window. Arvin raged and scooted away, but the gunman now looked defeated and nearly pathetic. No one was going to pay any attention to his threats in his present condition, least of all the massive Jan Kesselring.

'I'm trying to find you some medical help, Arvin,' Jim told the prisoner, but all that earned him was a growl of complaint.

'I'll be right out here,' Jim told the smith, 'if you need me.'

Kesselring, holding a heavy hammer in his meaty hand, only grinned.

Jim stepped back toward his desk only to hear

another knock at the front door – a smaller, almost tentative tap. What now?

Walking that way he swung the door wide to find the small figure of Ginnie Cummings standing on the porch. Her eyes were shy, her mouth bashful.

'I still needed to talk to you . . .' she said hesitantly. 'I don't know if this is a good time.' She shifted her eyes to the cell where the ringing of Kesselring's hammer was sounding.

'It's as good as any,' Jim said to the blonde waitress. 'We're just trying to finish up a few things that had to be done around here. Come in. Sit down.'

Ginnie, wearing jeans and a blue flannel shirt, crossed the room toward the desk, noticing that there was only one chair in the room. Jim remembered that the other had been given to Arvin.

'Sit down,' Jim repeated. 'Tell me what's on your mind.'

'I won't be long,' Ginnie promised. 'It's just that I have a small problem.'

'Marshal!' Jan Kesselring's voice interrupted. Jim held up a finger for patience and walked to the cell where Kesselring was working. Arvin Hinton sat slumped against the floor in the corner of the room.

'What is it, Jan?' Jim asked, slightly annoyed at the intrusion.

'Just wanted to remind you that the other chair is in here. This bird won't need it after I get these cot chains pinned to the wall.'

'No, I guess not,' Jim said, still perturbed. He swung the chair toward the office. Kesselring stopped him,

holding up a massive hand. The blacksmith bent
forward and said in a whisper:

'That's the woman, Marshal. I recognize her voice.
She's the one who brought that note about Dandy
Trout.'

Jim paused, stunned. 'No doubt about it?'

'No doubt at all.'

EIGHT

Jim Early looked into Kesselring's earnest eyes, trying to absorb what he had been told.

Ginnie Cummings had delivered the note that had lured Jim out to Trout's shack and gotten him ambushed? It seemed impossible. But Kesselring had been here at the time, in the same position as he was now when the woman left the letter.

Carrying the chair, Jim returned to his desk and sat behind it, offering Ginnie the other seat. He studied her blue-gray eyes, the shyness of her mouth, her nervous hands, which seemed to be searching for a place to settle. The woman was upset about something, that was for sure.

'Tell me about it,' Jim said, leaning forward, forearms on the desk.

Ginnie began hesitantly, almost by rote as if it were some story memorized, and as she went along, growing more nervous, Jim became convinced that that was exactly what it was – an elaborate lie. He watched, puzzled, and listened carefully to what he was being told.

'I live alone, Jim. I have a small place north of town. It's only forty acres, but there's good water and graze. My brother Toby and I started it on money my parents left us. We thought we could make a go of it. We wanted to raise horses. There's no one else in the area who does that. Last spring, however, Toby was killed. I don't know who did it or why, but I learned quickly that I could no longer manage the ranch on my own.

'I had to find other work and fast. That's how I ended up at Ethel M's.

'The recent trouble at the ranch has threatened to leave me nothing – no future at all.' She snuffled a little and continued. 'One morning I found that someone had opened my chicken pen and let all of my brood hens out. I used to be able to count on egg money from those hens; now. . . .'

Jim watched her steadily. Her eyes met his once and flickered away. Jan's hammering had stopped in the cell. 'Go on,' Jim said.

'The other night my dog was killed as it roamed the yard, and the next morning I discovered that two of my best colts had been run off the ranch. The profit I had hoped to make from them was gone. It seemed I was doomed to lose the ranch and become a drudge at Ethel M's for the rest of my foreseeable life.

'Last night,' Ginnie said, 'I spotted two men out in the yard where the horse pen stands. I fired one angry shot at them, but hit nothing. The men ran away, but they'll be back, I'm sure – maybe to burn the house down, maybe to do worse!'

Her eyes, Jim noticed, were now misted. She held a small lace handkerchief to her face.

He drummed his fingers on the desktop and leaned back in his chair. Looking levelly at her, he asked, 'Is any of that true, Ginnie?'

She broke down completely, her head bowed, her shoulders trembling. From behind her handkerchief, she murmured, 'Some of it. My brother's dead.'

'I see. Was it true that you knew Dandy Trout had my stolen money?'

'I was told he did. . . .' Whatever else she had started to say was washed away in a flood of tearful hiccups. Jim had wanted to like the woman, wanted to believe her, but now the tears did nothing to touch him. He had lived too long with a woman who was expert at dispensing tears when the occasion called for it. Linda Lu was much more adept at such artifices than this small-town girl.

Jim wondered. The girl was trying to protect herself, or something, or someone, with lies. Who, what, and why?

He asked, 'What was I supposed to do? Go out to your ranch in the night to give them a second crack at me? I very nearly got shot dead today; the little man, Dandy Trout, did get himself killed. Why, Ginnie? Why would you involve yourself in something so devious?'

'Because . . .' she sniffled, 'because I am going to lose everything if I don't go along with him. Everything my brother and I tried to build up.'

'Go along with who?' Jim asked. 'If you don't go

along with *who?*'

'Frank Gerard, of course. I thought you'd have guessed by now.'

Frank Gerard. But he was the one who had pushed to have Jim hired for the marshal's job. Why would Gerard want to have him killed now?

'What you're telling me makes no sense,' Jim said to the hunched figure of the girl sitting opposite him.

'Don't you see?' Ginnie asked in a pleading voice. 'Frank Gerard holds the lien on my ranch. He owns half of everything around Zanzibar, and he wants more. He said if I'd do him one little favor – simply bringing a letter over to your office – he would give me an extension on my mortgage.'

'Did he say why he wanted me out of town?'

'He said,' Ginnie faltered, 'that he had the intention of spending some … time . . . with Linda Finch, and didn't want you around.'

'So he sent me out to be gunned down, with your assistance!' Jim said harshly.

'I didn't know that anything like that was going to happen,' she protested.

'No. Of course you didn't. Do you know why, Ginnie? You are a stupid girl, a stupid, stupid woman,' he said roughly.

Her face was buried in her hands. 'I know I am. I never thought so before, but I am stupid. Angry, confused, desperate, frantic and . . . stupid.'

Just then, Kesselring, making more noise than seemed necessary, emerged from the cell, toting his tools, and Jim rose to lock the door.

Kesselring, who must have heard most of the conversation, avoided looking at Ginnie Cummings. He only said, 'I'll have my cousin, Warren, come over to see you tomorrow. That is, if you are still wanting a new deputy.'

'I am. I'll be happy to see him. You might mention that this job will involve a lot of night work.'

'I'll tell him that, but the way things are around Zanzibar just now, he'll be happy for any opportunity. The town is being run into the ground, and it seems that everyone is fine with that as long as they're getting their own now.'

Grumbling, Kesselring went out. Moments later Bernie Tibbs came in the back door, slipping a little on the step. He glanced at Ginnie Cummings, but did not react. He told Jim, 'I found Ben Lovesy at the Red Bird. He was mostly sober but looking thirsty. He says he'll be along to look at the prisoner's wound.' Bernie raised an eyebrow. 'He'll be expecting some pay. But says he doesn't do amputations.'

'He'll be paid,' Jim answered, deliberately ignoring Ginnie while he took care of office business. From the cell an anguished voice called out, 'Amputation!' No one responded to Arvin Hinton's cry.

'Oh, also, Boss,' Bernie Tibbs said, sitting in Jim's chair behind the desk, 'Matt and Andy are already on their way to take care of. . . .' Tibbs broke off with uncommon deference. 'You know?'

'See that the little man gets a decent burial,' Jim said coldly, looking hard at Ginnie, who lifted her eyes in a brief flicker and then shifted them quickly away again.

'You still going to see the judge?' Bernie asked,

110

looking greedily at his bottle. He wanted Jim to leave; that was obvious. The worst drunks prefer to drink in private where there are no accusing eyes.

'Yes, and I'd better get going,' Jim said. 'Do you still have Arvin's pistol?'

'Of course. Right here in the desk drawer.'

'All right. Keep it handy and keep the doors locked,' he said as a remorseful Ginnie Cummings rose from her chair, having gotten the hint that it was time to leave. 'We still have no idea what Billy Hinton might have in mind.'

'All right, boss.'

'Don't let anyone in, and stay here!'

'I've got no reason to go out,' Bernie said, tapping the whiskey bottle in front of him.

'I'll try to send some food over for you and the prisoner,' Jim promised.

'I can do that,' Ginnie said. Her expression was that of a pup or a small child trying to make amends for misconduct. Jim grumbled his assent.

Evening was settling as he stepped out on to the plank walk in front of the jail, feeling weary and well-used. Ginnie followed him through the door, and Jim waited for the sound of Bernie Tibbs turning the key in the lock.

'I guess he'll handle things well enough,' Jim said mostly to himself as he turned uptown toward Judge O'Connell's office, Ginnie hurrying along beside and a little behind him.

'They're roasting pork at Ethel M's tonight,' she said, looking up at the fast-moving marshal. 'Maybe I should bring their meals over myself tonight so that Bernie doesn't get nervous.'

'Bernie doesn't get nervous at this time of the evening. Do it yourself or not. I really don't care at all.'

'Still mad?'

'Of course I am. You sent me out to have me assassinated. I liked you, Ginnie. I really did. I even believed that I could trust you – what a fool a man can be.'

'Jim?' He felt her fingers gripping the fabric of his shirt and he stopped, scowling down at her in the dimness of settling dusk. 'I'd like to know about ... Linda Finch – did you kiss her a lot?'

Still wondering at the caprices of a woman's mind, Jim Early tramped toward the judge's office, which was on the second floor above a shop named Brenda's Necessaries and Notions. Jim had seen lantern light from below and so he knew the judge was still in.

He tapped at the door and was summoned.

'Ah, Marshal Travers,' the man behind the desk said. 'I was wondering when we would have the chance to talk.'

'It's time,' Jim said. In the dim light cast by the flickering lantern, he saw a rail-thin man with dark hair slicked back, wearing smoked glasses, which concealed his eyes completely, on the bridge of a hawkish nose.

Smoked glasses were rare; Jim had only seen a blind man or two wearing such things. He hesitated as he approached the judge. 'I can see you well enough,' O'Connell assured him. 'I once spent too much time in the sun.'

That could have meant anything from catching the

glare off the white land to having been staked out in the sun. Jim hadn't come to question the man concerning his past.

'Mind if I take a seat?' he asked.

'You'd better; this may take us a while,' O'Connell said with an expression that was not quite a smile.

'I hope not too long. I don't want to waste your time,' Jim said.

'Time has little value; it is only a commodity for those who wish to buy some back, which of course they cannot.'

Jim only nodded and seated himself. He was here on practical matters. Not for philosophical discussion.

The judge said, 'I think I can guess what's on your mind. What authority do I have, do you have, on the streets of Zanzibar? Who is committing crimes and who is not when our statutes are not just ill-written, but unwritten? In fact, there is no law in Zanzibar.'

'That's exactly it,' Jim agreed. 'I don't have any idea what laws I am supposed to enforce, not knowing that they are.'

'Like staggering blindly, is it not?' the judge asked, smiling to himself. Leaning back in his chair, O'Connell cupped a painfully thin knee in his hands and looked toward the ceiling. 'The way things are now arranged, we will have to wait until the mayor and town council have presented specific and enforceable statutes to me. I have no idea what they might be considering.'

'Except running Colin Pippen out of town and closing down the Red Bird Saloon,' Jim said sourly.

'That won't happen,' the judge said, dropping his feet forward to the floor in a sudden movement. 'That might be among their intentions, but I won't allow it on baseless grounds. Look, Marshal Travers, we have to be on the same side or confusion will reign. Here is my thinking. The Red Bird may be a nuisance to the town council, but it has as much right to exist as their own businesses. They may have a point about all-night drinking at the Red Bird; we might have to establish a closing hour. Drunken fights and vandalism have been a problem, I agree. I have no objection to those men having a good time, but when it disrupts the town's peace and safety, common sense tells me that it should be limited in some way.'

'Have you talked to Colin Pippen about this?' Jim asked.

The judge frowned, sucked at his lower lip, and asked, 'Have you ever met Colin Pippen?'

'Yes, I have.'

'And how was he to talk to?' the judge asked.

'Difficult,' Jim admitted.

'Exactly. Pippen wants things the way they have always been; the town council wants everything changed to exactly the way they wish it to be.'

'Still, you'd think a compromise could be worked out,' Jim suggested.

'I think it could – with Peter Wiley and Hazlitt, that is. Not with Frank Gerard, never.'

'Why is that?' Jim asked, believing he already knew the answer.

'The Red Bird is the biggest moneymaker in town by

far. Frank Gerard has squandered a lot of money on his various enterprises, like constructing cottages that will have no buyers in the foreseeable future. He wants the Red Bird, by fair means or foul.'

Outside, the evening had grown pleasantly cool. There was some sort of ruckus down at the Red Bird, but there was no shooting and Jim didn't think it was worth his while to investigate. The one thing his conversation with Judge O'Connell had solidified was that most of Zanzibar's troubles didn't originate with the Red Bird Saloon, but with Frank Gerard and his desire to own the profitable enterprise. Was that why Jim had been given the marshal's job after all – as a hired gun?

How could he not be grateful to Gerard for giving him a place to live and a job? Well, Jim wasn't grateful. Especially after listening to Judge O'Connell, who certainly knew more about the affairs of Zanzibar than he did, and seemed certain of his facts. And after listening to Ginnie Cummings, who seemed to have been forced into a bind by Frank Gerard in which she was to play the game his way or lose her little ranch. Jim wasn't used to such deviousness. The men he met were usually either good or bad, but straightforward about it.

And where was Linda Lu just then? Gerard seemed to be showering attention on her. Although Jim knew that Linda had experience fending off such men, he was uncertain and unhappy with the situation. After all, if Ginnie's ploy had worked, Gerard would expect Jim Early to be out at her ranch on this evening, watching

for trouble, not at home with Linda. Jim recovered his
gray horse and rode for home, a little more swiftly than
he normally would have.

NINE

Linda's buggy was in front of the house, but her bay horse had been put away. There was no other animal in evidence. Jim rode to the front hitch rail, swung down, and loosened the cinches on his saddle, silently promising the gray that he would return soon to see to it properly.

He called out, tramped up the porch to the front door, and swung it wide.

Linda Lu was sitting on the new blue sofa, fiddling with her fingernails. 'You make enough noise,' she said without looking up.

'I'm sorry,' Jim said, going behind her to gently rub her neck. 'I just wanted to let you know I was coming.'

'I knew you were coming, Jim,' Linda said, turning a smile in his direction. 'What's troubling you?'

'Frank Gerard is troubling me,' he said, seating himself opposite her on a blue upholstered chair.

'You mean the funny man with the big red mustache?' Linda asked.

'You know who I mean,' Jim replied. 'I thought he might be here.'

'He was,' Linda said, hiding a yawn behind her well-manicured hand. 'I sent him packing.'

'He wasn't bothering you, was he?' Jim asked.

'Men don't have that kind of power over me, you know that, Jim. He was a little annoying and quite boring, but that's all.'

'You mean he didn't try anything?'

'Of course he did,' Linda said languidly, as if it were a daily occurrence in her life, which, of course, it was.

'And. . . ?'

'I told you, I sent him packing. I told him he was a bore and that if you got home before he was gone, you'd likely blow his ass off.'

Jim smiled despite himself. Linda was likely to pop out with crude expressions at odd times. She didn't even seem to know they were crude. They were a part of the vocabulary of the world she had been brought up in.

She leaned forward and took Jim's hands. 'You know you don't have to worry about things like that, Jim. But there's more bothering you, isn't there? Tell me about it. We didn't get our money back, I can tell by your expression; but what else happened?'

Jim did. He told Linda Lu all about his day – his first day as the marshal of Zanzibar. He told her about Arvin, about having to shoot him and lock him up in the new jail, about receiving the mysterious note and riding out to Dandy Trout's shack only to find Trout dead, about the ambush on the way back to town. He told her about talking with Colin Pippen and meeting with Judge O'Connell, about borrowing more money from Hazlitt;

he told her what he had heard from the judge and others concerning Frank Gerard's business affairs and the way he handled them.

He told her about Ginnie Cummings.

Finished, he leaned back and looked up at the woman with the liquid brown eyes. The corners of Linda's mouth twitched and she said, 'Little man, you've had a busy day.' Jim wanted to laugh, but could not. Relating all of his problems had brought them too vividly to mind. Linda reached across and nudged his shoulder. She was still smiling.

'A blonde, huh?'

It took Jim a minute to realize who she was referring to. Out of all that he had told her, Linda had picked the least important point to comment on. Women's thought processes continued to amaze him, probably always would.

'Maybe you should go out to the girl's ranch to check on her, Jim. Poor little thing living there all alone.' There was not-so-subtle mockery in Linda's voice, but it was good-natured.

'The only thing threatening her is Frank Gerard,' Jim mumbled. He ran his fingers through his coppery hair. 'This is so involved, I don't know where to begin. It's just a tangled mess.'

Linda leaned back, looking very feline just then. She folded her long legs under her and examined her painted fingernails again. Glancing at Jim, she asked, 'What part don't you understand, Jim? It all seems pretty obvious to me.'

She was quite serious and quite sure of herself. Jim's

119

eyebrows folded together as he studied her. 'If you know, why don't you tell me?'

'All right,' Linda said, and without any doubt in her voice, she calmly explained. 'Of course this has been a set-up from the beginning. A pretty much down-on-his-luck man with a gunfighter's reputation – that's you, Jim – shows up in a town desperate for a willing gun hand. They wanted to approach you with the marshal's job, but first they had to make sure you were truly desperate. They set out to bilk you at a card game, hiring this Ben Lytle, who doesn't seem to have been very good at his job.'

'I've seen better. I knew when to lay off the betting,' Jim said.

'Yes.' Linda stretched her arms overhead again. 'You told me that Lytle complained about how far in debt he was. That's why he needed the money.'

'He did.'

'And I think he was, yet he kept on playing. Someone had to have given him those thousands of dollars to gamble with in case things went bad at first. That would be the man Lytle was in debt to, the man to whom he owed a favor, and the man who wanted to be sure that you were pressed into a corner and would have to take the offered marshal's job.'

'Frank Gerard?' Jim asked.

'Of course. But Lytle proved to be too clumsy as a card shark and by the time the game had played out, you had twenty thousand dollars of *Gerard's* money. Lytle panicked; there was no telling what Frank Gerard would do to him. He felt like he had to steal the money back.

'When he ran down the street he passed the money off to someone – maybe an unsuspecting Dandy Trout, or more probably to Gerard himself. Then Gerard had you where he wanted you. You had no choice but to take the marshal's job or hit the long trail with your fancy lady, who would not willingly do that. I know,' Linda said with a strange smile.

Jim replied, 'Say this is what happened. After I took the job, someone – Gerard, it seems – decided to have me killed. Why? After all that work trying to force me into it?'

'Because you seemed determined to do the job right instead of just running Colin Pippen out of town – remember, the Red Bird was always Gerard's chief objective. You continued to search for your stolen money, which Gerard had and needed because of his business losses, and,' Linda paused, 'your replacement was already on the way.'

'Kyle Colson?'

'Of course. A ruthless gunfighter, from all accounts, who would have nothing against using his guns to drive Colin Pippen out of business. Who was there to oppose Colson but you?'

'The man has a crooked mind!' Jim said.

'Gerard? Of course he does. He pressured this girl – Ginnie Cummings, is it?'

'You know it is. You never miss a thing.'

'Yes. He pressured the blonde into luring you out to Trout's shack where either Colson or more likely Gerard himself tried to finish you off.'

'I don't understand why Ginnie would agree to that,'

121

Jim said.

Linda noticed the look in his eyes. Yes, he liked the blonde girl. 'It was a man she barely knew in exchange for her ranch and all of the hopes she has for now and for the future, Jim.' Her voice softened. 'She might not have even had an idea what was in the note. She was told to deliver it and did.'

'And all this time he's also duping his partners, Peter Wiley and Mayor Hazlitt, who seem to actually want to clean Zanzibar up for decent citizens.' Jim shook his head heavily. Wasn't that exactly what Judge O'Connell had suggested?

Jim rose to his feet and looked around the now well-furnished cabin. 'All of this! He didn't have to do all of this to convince me to stay, did he?'

'Oh, this!' Linda said with a short laugh. 'That wasn't for you, Jim. It was all done for me. When you were gone, killed, who would I have to turn to but the man who has been so good to me?'

'Why, that slimy. . . .' Jim's vocabulary failed him.

'Whatever word you were looking for, that's what he is,' Linda said. 'One of the man's problems is that he thinks so much of himself that he can't understand anyone not agreeing with his assessment. I've known a lot of men like him, Jim. You know that. Most of them had bigger plans, more resources, were smarter than Frank Gerard, but they run to type.'

'I wonder what I should do,' Jim said, sagging on to the chair again.

'Probably nothing but continue to do the best job you can for the town,' Linda said with conviction.

'I suppose you're right. I've gotten a new office and a jail cell. I've got a line on a new deputy, one who's sober and willing to work. I've got Judge O'Connell on my side – at least partially. All I have to do is keep an eye open for Kyle Colson and for Billy Hinton. I'd like to talk to Colin Pippen again about making some compromises in the way he does business. That might be enough to satisfy Wiley and Hazlitt.'

'But not Gerard.'

'Of course not. Not if he covets the Red Bird.'

'You know, Jim,' Linda said in a soft but taunting voice, 'it seems that you are really starting to care about your job, about this shanty town. Don't forget what your main purpose is – we have to have that money.'

'I know we do,' Jim said quietly. Twenty thousand dollars and the road to Santa Fe lay open to them. Somewhere Linda could be truly happy and Jim would not have to worry about lurking guns.

'Let's go to bed,' he said, suddenly rising.

'Good idea – I have to get up early tomorrow anyway,' Linda replied as Jim tugged her up from the sofa.

'Oh?' he said as he hugged her.

'Yes. I'm going to breakfast with Frank Gerard.'

He wondered briefly if she was kidding, but he knew Linda well enough to know she was not. They were safe enough for tonight. They could sleep well without fear of gunmen or fire. Gerard would never risk having Linda Lu hit in a crossfire of bullets, nor would he let a valuable piece of his property be burned out.

It was strange comfort.

The big kid was sitting in front of Jim's office when he got there shortly before eight o'clock the following morning. As he rose to greet Jim, he drew himself to his full height. He was not big, he was huge. Warren Dodge was a freak of nature. Jim let the man introduce himself although there was no doubt who Kesselring's cousin was. He shook hands quickly and tentatively, not wanting his hand to be crushed in the big man's grip. Dodge's face was boyish and round. It didn't look as if he needed to shave as yet. His smile was affable.

'I knocked once on the door, but no one answered,' Dodge said. 'So I sat down to wait for you. Marshal,' he said earnestly, 'I really could use a job if you'd be willing to take me on and give me a trial.'

'That's what we'll do,' Jim said as he unlocked the door. In his mind he had already hired Warren Dodge. Where else was he to find such an eager young deputy?

Inside the jail Arvin Hinton was moaning and whimpering on his new, chain-hung bunk, and in Jim's chair, tilted back against the wall, Bernie Tibbs sat with his feet on the desk, a tipped-over bottle on the floor beside him. Jim awakened Bernie with a shake of the shoulder. The narrow man sat up, rubbing his arms.

'Mornin', Marshal,' Bernie said around a yawn. His red eyes focused on Warren Dodge.

'Who's this?' he asked sleepily.

'He's my new deputy, the man who's going to take your place,' Jim said.

Bernie Tibbs' reaction was a resigned smile and a

thin shrug. 'I take it I'm fired, then?'

'I'm going to have to let you go – you knew your job was only temporary when you took it.'

'Yup,' Bernie answered. 'And it's just as well as far as I'm concerned.' He rose shakily, rubbing his back. 'This job is all right, but it sure makes a man stiff overnight. I'm better off at my old routine.' He searched around for his battered hat, finding it also on the floor. Placing the torn hat on his head, he said, 'I did get Ben Lovesy to come over and take a look at the prisoner, and I guess he did his best, but he didn't hold out much hope for that ankle healing properly. Said the man will always have a limp.'

'The price of crime,' Jim said, still feeling little sympathy for Arvin Hinton, his old partner who had elected to shoot him down.

'Yes, well, I'll be on my way, Marshal.' Bernie's watery eyes became hopeful as he looked around the office. 'I did my best, you know. If you ever need temporary help again. . . .'

It was obvious that Tibbs was just dragging the conversation along. Jim slipped the man two silver dollars from the town fund and Bernie brightened and headed for the back door of the office.

'He seems like a good man,' Warren Dodge said. It was indicative of his good nature.

'Well, I've got to say that he did everything I asked of him,' Jim reflected.

'That's just what I intend to do, Marshal,' the big kid said sincerely.

'Did you bring a gun with you?' Jim asked, settling

into his chair.

'No, sir. I didn't know if you'd be hiring me or not. Anyway, I don't own a short gun. Never had no use for one before.'

Jim opened the top desk drawer. Arvin Hinton's slick Colt .44 with the stag-handle grips was still there. He spun it across the desk in the direction of Dodge. 'You can have this one.'

Dodge looked at the pistol admiringly and then tucked it behind his belt. 'Do I need a badge as well?' the giant asked.

'We're kind of short on badges. There's only this one,' Jim said, tapping the shield on his leather vest.

Warren Dodge looked vaguely disappointed. Jim unpinned his own badge and told him, 'You might as well wear this one. Most everyone in town knows who I am anyway.'

'Thanks, Marshal,' Dodge said, pinning the badge to his red shirt. 'What do you want me to do first?' He looked around as if he had broom work in mind, and the place could use some sweeping out. Kesselring's residue still dusted the floor. Instead Jim told Dodge:

'Why don't you just walk up and down the street a little; let men see you and realize I've got a new deputy. On your way back, if you don't mind, you might stop in at Ethel M's and grab some breakfast for me and our prisoner – hotcakes and sausage will be fine.' Jim passed a few silver coins over. 'If you want, have yourself some breakfast while you're there – if you haven't already had it.'

'No, I haven't. Thank you, Marshal, really.' Warren

Dodge looked surprised, gratified, and proud at once. So far the big kid seemed to see this job as a stroke of luck.

Arvin was moaning in his cell and with a shooing gesture, Jim sent Dodge on his way and went to peer through the bars on the window of the cell door at the unhappy ex-con.

'What's the matter now, Arvin?' Jim asked.

'The matter? I'm hurt, I'm hungry, I'm locked up for nothing.'

'I'm taking care of breakfast. If your ankle keeps on hurting I'll get Ben Lovesy back over here. He can saw it off pretty neatly.'

'You know what, Jim. I never thought you were—'

A pistol shot from outside interrupted Arvin's tirade. Darting to the front door, his own pistol in hand, Jim stepped cautiously out on to the boardwalk. Men were starting toward the jail. A large, inert form in a red shirt and marshal's shield lay sprawled against the planks of the porch. It was Warren Dodge and he had been shot in the chest, the bullet entering just inches from his new silver badge.

127

TEN

There was no reason for it. Jim crouched down next to the fallen Warren Dodge, trying to staunch the flow of blood with his bandanna. Men were crowding around asking questions. He knew most of them. None had a reason to shoot Dodge. It had to be someone who didn't know the kid and mistakenly thought, because of the badge on his shirt, that he was the town marshal. These thoughts flickered through Jim's mind as he tried and failed to halt the flow of blood from Dodge's chest.

Jim knew a few of the faces among the crowded bystanders, including Tyler Hough and Junior Weber. Junior had a beer mug in his hand. Jim snarled at them. 'Help me get him inside. Somebody run and get Ben Lovesy, and tell him to bring his tools; this man needs help!'

From around the corner of the alleyway, Bernie Tibbs appeared, bottle in hand. He came forward with a drunkard's shamble, looked at the fallen Warren Dodge and asked Jim, 'Does this mean you want me on again – temporary?'

'You're on again,' Jim grumbled as the two men he had asked tried to lift the massive fallen deputy and get him inside the office. Jim glanced at the whiskered, shaky Bernie Tibbs. He wasn't much, but he would need someone to watch the office while he went hunting.

Hunting for the man who had tried to kill Warren Dodge.

There being no bed inside the office, Dodge was placed on the floor in a corner with a folded blanket for a pillow. The kid was incapable of speech although his eyes were partly open and his lips did twitch slightly. Hough and Weber didn't wait around for thanks or a reward; they were off, back to the Red Bird where the gossip of the day would be swirling hotly.

Jim handed Arvin's pistol back to Bernie Tibbs. 'You know the routine – no one in here except Ben Lovesy, though I don't know what he can do for the kid.'

'Probably nothing amazing,' Bernie answered, placing his bottle down on the desk, 'but you have to reckon how many bullet wounds Ben saw in his five years of war as a surgeon's assistant.'

'What's happening?' Arvin Hinton shouted from his cell. Perhaps he thought his brother, Billy, had tried to stage a jailbreak. Jim ignored the prisoner. He squatted beside Dodge, still trying and failing to stem the flow of blood from the young man's chest.

The front door to the office was flung open and Jim turned automatically that way, hand going to his holstered Colt.

'Jim!'

It was Ginnie Cummings who stood in the doorway, wearing her waitress's outfit, the cuffs of her blue jeans still showing beneath the hem of the dark skirt. She looked at the blood-soaked bandanna in his hand, then into his eyes and stammered, 'Oh ... you're all right? They were talking in the restaurant, said the marshal had been gunned down in the street.' She was breathing hard. She must have run all the way from Ethel M's. Why? Only yesterday she'd had a hand in trying to have Jim Early killed.

Her eyes were wide with concern, bright with emotion.

'Sit down, Ginnie,' Jim said with a roughness he did not feel. The girl was weaving on her feet. 'It wasn't me, it was Warren Dodge who was shot.'

'Warren?' She seemed only now to notice the big man on the floor, Bernie hovering over him. 'Why?'

'Because he was wearing a badge,' Jim said grimly.

It was then that the door admitted the small, shaky figure of Ben Lovesy. He showed signs of drink, too, but there was little else to choose from in Zanzibar. Lovesy had his battered leather medical satchel in his hand.

'Just the one customer?' the little white-haired man inquired.

'Just the one,' Jim answered. 'Do what you can for him.'

'I'll give it my best try. Same pay rate?'

'Whatever I gave you for the prisoner and more if you can get that bullet out.'

'We'll see about that – it's not my specialty, but I'll try.' Ben Lovesy noticed Ginnie Cummings and said to her, 'You probably don't want to see this, miss.'

'No,' she said hesitantly, 'I suppose I don't.'

'Breakfast!' Arvin Hinton yelled from his cell and Jim asked Ginnie:

'Can you have something to eat sent over?'

'For how many?' Ginnie looked the men over.

'The prisoner and,' Jim looked long at his tipsy deputy, 'Bernie. Only two meals.'

'What about you, Jim?' Ginnie asked gently. There was moisture in her eyes again, concern.

He shook his head. 'I'm going out. I won't be back for a while.'

Perhaps for a very long while.

Exiting a minute after Ginnie as Ben Lovesy hunched over the wounded Warren Dodge, Bernie standing by looking useless, Jim heard himself hailed from across the street.

Mayor Hazlitt stood in front of his store, waving an arm toward Jim. 'Marshal! What's happened? Where are you going?'

Jim kept on walking. If Hazlitt wanted a report he could have one later, and it would probably be more informative than Hazlitt would like. Because the mayor had to be told about Frank Gerard. Whatever Jim told him would probably come as no great surprise, but no one likes to have his worst suspicions confirmed.

Jim's mind was fixed only on one objective now – finding Kyle Colson and dealing with the gunfighter. Colson was a reputed killer and supposed to be a wizard with a six-shooter. But then, Jim thought, he himself had a reputation as a fast gunhand, built mostly on hearsay and rumor. Maybe Colson's own reputation wasn't as represented. After all, he had not faced Warren Dodge boldly in the street but had shot him down from hiding.

No matter. He had to face Colson. What good was a marshal who avoided trouble? It was the surest way to lose all support in a town like Zanzibar. In any town.

Where to begin looking for Colson? The man had ridden into town, and might be considering riding out now if he believed that he had finished the job he was hired to do. He had to have been keeping his horse somewhere. Jim decided to start looking at the Joker Stable. He was now acquainted with the brothers Matt and Andy Pierce, having used them to bury Dandy Trout. He thought they would tell him the truth; neither had a reason to protect Kyle Colson.

Andy Pierce was standing at the open stable doors, hands on his hips, face intent when Jim arrived. 'You just missed him,' was the first thing the dark-eyed Andy said.

'Missed who?'

'Why, aren't you after that gunfighter? The one who killed Warren Dodge?'

'Warren's not dead,' Jim told him. Not yet. News just flew around this town. 'But someone tried to kill him. I think he mistook Warren for me.'

'I know he did!' Andy said excitedly. 'He came in, asked for his pinto pony, and couldn't help bragging how he had outdrawn and outshot our big town marshal. I didn't say anything; you don't like to challenge such men, but I knew from his description that it wasn't you he shot, and I knew Warren was thinking of hiring on with you. I couldn't see Warren Dodge getting into a gunfight with Kyle Colson. He isn't that kind of man.'

'He didn't,' Jim said as they walked into the stables toward where Jim's gray horse stood in its stall. 'And Kyle Colson didn't beat anyone in a stand-up fight. Warren was shot before he even knew what was happening. His gun was still behind his belt.'

'Why, that dirty . . . big gunhand, huh!' Andy scoffed.

'Which way did he go, Andy?' Jim asked as the stablehand swung the saddle on to the gray's back.

'I watched him for a way – he was heading south toward Bedel Road.'

Jim nodded. That would figure. There was water there for his horse and Trout's cabin was a good place to hide out – or to meet with someone else. Maybe Colson and Frank Gerard had agreed to meet there after the gunfighter had taken care of Jim Early. Both knew where the cabin was; it was where Dandy Trout had been killed and Jim ambushed. There was little doubt that one or both of these men was responsible for that. With the marshal of Zanzibar dead, as he believed, Kyle Colson could wait without fear at the cabin. He knew Zanzibar well enough to know that no one was going to raise a posse in this town.

'I'll see if I can cut his sign,' Jim said, swinging aboard the gray, 'but I've no doubt you're right. Thanks, Andy.'

'Just take care of the bastard, Marshal. Warren Dodge is a good old boy.'

Jim nodded and rode out into the cool light of day. Take care of Kyle Colson? He wasn't sure that he could, but he meant to try his best. Riding steadily southward Jim wondered if he would be so fortunate as to find Frank Gerard at Trout's shack. That would give him all the proof he needed to accuse Gerard. Gerard must have been informed by now that the man Colson had been paid to shoot was not Jim Early at all but an innocent man, Warren Dodge. That could cause the meeting between the two to turn ugly. Perhaps Gerard, figuring he had not gotten service for his money, would decline to ride out to meet Colson at all, leaving Colson angry and vindictive.

There was no telling and no point in pondering it all. Jim let the gray horse plod along at its chosen gait toward Trout's cabin. He was in no hurry. He had found the tracks of Colson's horse at the outskirts of town and Colson was not travelling fast, either. Why would he? What did he have to fear? Well, Jim told himself, arrogance had led more than one man to his destruction. As for a plan, Jim had none but to ride carefully and keep his eyes moving. He silently cursed Frank Gerard. If the man had just let Jim keep his legal winnings, he would not find himself now in this position. He and Linda would be long gone from Zanzibar and back in civilization.

With the sun nearly overhead Jim came upon the cot-tonwood grove. The pond beyond was gleaming like polished steel in the bright light of day. The shack where Trout had lived appeared squat, crooked, and deserted, although it was not. Jim saw the tethered pinto horse lift its head. Then it nickered, and Jim smothered a curse.

He barely had time to draw his pistol before a man burst from the cabin. His eyes were wild. He wore a very thin, drooping mustache. His jaw was square, his face the dull pallor of white cheese. This had to be the gun-fighter Kyle Colson. To accentuate the point the running man winged a shot at Jim, who leaned to the side of the gray. The bullet whined off the trees behind him, and sang into the distances.

Rather than stand and fight, Colson started his pony forward and mounted it on the run, fleeing the shelter of the cottonwoods. Jim had no clear shot as the man passed among the trees. He hadn't expected the expe-rienced gunman to flee, but his sudden appearance seemed to have unnerved Colson. Plus, in his mind, Colson had just killed the town marshal of Zanzibar, and seemed to think the town might feel a hanging was in order.

As Jim cleared the woods and reached the pond, Colson had ridden his horse in a splashing, mad dash for escape into the water. The gunfighter now turned and fired wildly at Jim. The shots whipped past him, coming very close, but as Colson fired awkwardly from the back of a floundering horse, none was truly aimed.

Jim braced himself and fired twice. One .44 slug

entered each of Colson's shoulders, bringing a howl of pain from the panicked, fleeing outlaw. With two injured arms, Colson lost control of his horse and toppled from its back, splashing into the pond. The pinto ran on.

Jim formed a hasty loop with his lariat and threw it toward Colson, missing his mark. He was too long out of practice, he decided. Re-forming the loop of damp rope, he tried again. Colson still flailed his arms in a vain attempt to make his escape by swimming. After another minute and another missed toss by Jim, the motion ceased. Colson's activity had turned his body so that now Jim had a clear view of the killer's feet and he managed to loop them both with a neat toss he would have been proud of under other circumstances. He tightened the noose and then, sure of his capture, he backed the gray slowly from the bank of the pond, towing Kyle Colson shoreward.

By the time the horse had backed to the verge of the cottonwood grove, Colson had been dragged ashore. Jim cautiously approached the still figure lying there in the wet sand. There was no need for caution. Jim's shots had not been killing ones, but Colson was dead by drowning. Jim had not been hit by a single bullet although Colson had been spraying a lot of lead around. He stood over Colson's inert form, looking at the reputed killer. Colson's blind eyes showed nothing of the fire, the hate that had filled his life. There was no more life in them than in those of a beached fish. Such do legends pass.

Jim waited near the cabin for a long hour. There had

been no money on the killer's body and so he had obviously come to the cabin to wait for his pay from Frank Gerard. There was no other reason for a man on the run to pause here and let himself be trapped inside a shack. But if Jim had guessed right, Frank Gerard already knew that it was Warren Dodge who had been shot and not Jim Early, and he would not pay a bounty to Colson for that mistake.

Jim knew that he had to put his case strongly not only to Gerard, but to the rest of the city council and Judge O'Connell. None of them could be so blind as to not reach the conclusion Jim had when faced with the evidence.

Frank Gerard was finished in Zanzibar.

Jim considered what to do with the body of Kyle Colson; it could not be left to rot. However, he felt no obligation toward Colson as he had for Dandy Trout and didn't wish to carry his corpse back to Zanzibar like some sort of hunter's trophy. Colson's pinto had gone and was presumably still running. He didn't wish to use the gray as a charnel horse again; the animal didn't deserve such treatment. Jim decided that he would have either Andy or Matt Pierce drive out here with a wagon and transport the body for burial. Colson wouldn't mind the wait.

Jim mounted his horse again and turned it toward Zanzibar. What was there left to do on this day? First he meant to check on Warren Dodge and find out how the big kid was doing. Then he was going to find Gerard, who should not be all that hard to track down. The man who owned half of Zanzibar was unlikely to just mount a horse and run out on to the long desert. He couldn't know that his gunfighter was lying dead on the banks of the pond and that his plot was about to be exposed. Somewhere along the way Jim would have to talk to Hazlitt and Wiley, and then Judge O'Connell would have to be advised so that proper legal action could be taken.

And where was Linda Lu? She had said she was going to breakfast with the man. Jim didn't want her around Gerard when he figured out what was happening and that arrest and prosecution was imminent. Men were unpredictable at such a moment.

Jim smiled as his stomach gurgled, reminding him that he had better find a few minutes along his way to eat something. For some reason – maybe because she was just beneath the surface of his thoughts – his need to eat reminded him of a certain blonde waitress at Ethel M's restaurant.

He wanted to talk to Ginnie in private and let her know that she had nothing left to fear from Frank Gerard; the man wouldn't be conducting any business for a long time to come.

Bernie Tibbs, unsurprisingly reeking of raw, hard liquor, was holding down the office. There were two empty platters on the desk, so both prisoner and deputy had eaten. In answer to Jim's question, Bernie told him, 'Warren's cousin, Jan Kesselring, and another man came over to take him home. Ben Lovesy was of the opinion that it couldn't hurt to move him, and besides it was better than leaving Warren on the hard floor.'

'Did Ben manage to get the bullet out?'

'Here it is,' Bernie said, showing Jim a barely mal-formed .44 slug. 'I'm keeping it so Warren will have a souvenir.'

Jim shook his head. He, himself, never understood why some people kept souvenirs of a painful event.

'Do you need to go anywhere?' Jim asked Tibbs.

'No. I went outside while Ben was here. I figured it was all right; besides, I couldn't hold it much longer. Why? Are you figuring on leaving again right away?'

'Yes. Yes, I am. I'd like to have all of this sorted out today, if possible.'

'All right,' Tibbs agreed. 'Ben Lovesy had my lunch sent over from the Red Bird,' he said, opening the desk drawer to reveal a fresh bottle of liquor, 'so I guess I'll survive.' He paused, a slack grin on his face. 'What about Kyle Colson? You're here, so I don't guess he's coming back to town.'

'He's returning one last time,' Jim said coldly. 'In the back of a wagon. Matt and Andy will be going out to get him.'

Bernie nodded. 'I see. Then the man wasn't quite as good a shot as he advertised.'

'Not quite,' Jim said.

That was enough time spent gabbing with Bernie Tibbs when there were other things to do. His main concern had been for Warren Dodge, but if Jan Kesselring had taken him home, the kid was presum-ably going to survive and was now in the best of hands. Jim took his badge from the desk and pinned it on once more.

Now it was time to try to wrap things up. To *try*,

139

because there was always a snarl in every plan a man could devise, as the poet with the wee mousie had reminded them all.

Anxious as Jim was to conclude his business, there was no sense in rushing into it unthinking. And no point in attempting it on an empty stomach. Leading his horse, he walked the length of the street toward Ethel M's restaurant with more than a few men's eyes following him.

ELEVEN

Ginnie Cummings was not at the restaurant, but they did have country-baked ham, fresh eggs and fried potatoes to ease Jim's disappointment. Where did he want to go first? He did not think that rushing headlong after Gerard was the best idea. Besides, he had no idea where the man was. Jim wasn't in the mood to talk to Peter Wiley, the mayor and the judge just yet. He had the feeling that they would raise some sort of caution or objection to slow him down. The judge may have wanted to hold back until he had investigated, heard the evidence, and drawn up a warrant. Gerard was a friend of Wiley and Hazlitt. They would have to be convinced of his guilt. No, it was better to inform them all afterward.

In the end, Jim decided to ride home first. It was near enough that little time would be wasted, and he wanted to make sure that Linda Lu would keep her distance. It wouldn't do to have her anywhere near Gerard when Jim arrested him. The shadows beneath the cottonwood trees were lengthening as he followed the road home. The day was late enough that the sun was already canting toward the far mountains to the west.

Linda's buggy was in front of the house, the horse unhitched. No other animal was around. Good; she was alone, then. He had not wanted to encounter Frank Gerard just yet, especially not in his own home.

He found Linda seated on the blue sofa wearing a peach-colored silk dress. Although she did not rise at his entrance, her eyes were bright with emotion and her lips were parted, ready to speak.

'Finally!' she said in a breathy voice. 'Sit down, I've got news for you.'

'Such as?' Jim asked warily. He never knew where Linda's mind would wander. But there was an urgency in her tone and he seated himself, waiting.

'Frank Gerard has our money,' Linda told him.

'Of course he does,' Jim replied. His cool tone did nothing to calm her excitement.

'I went out to his house with him,' Linda divulged. 'I told him that this cottage just wasn't up to my standards, and he invited me to see what a real house was like.'

'Trying to lure you to him?'

'I suppose so,' Linda said, waving an impatient hand in the air. 'Who cares what that unimportant little man had in mind? So we rode out there in the buggy and he invited me in. *I was so excited!*' Linda said mockingly. 'A house with wallpaper and paneling and a chandelier in the hallway. I never had seen such a fine place in my life!'

Linda stopped acting. 'I brushed past him and raced

through the house in my eagerness. I saw it under the bed in the master bedroom.'

'Dust?' Jim asked blandly, and Linda threw a pillow from the couch at him.

'No. A certain green bag with wooden handles, Jim. I saw him nudge it farther under the bed with his toe, but it was the same sort of bag you've described to me. The one that Ben Lytle stuffed our money in.'

'You can't be certain,' Jim cautioned.

'No, but after Frank thought I might have seen it, he immediately took me by the elbow and guided me out of the room to show me more of his marvelous house. I'm as sure as I can be, Jim, just by the way the man acted.'

'I'd better recover it before Gerard decides to hide it somewhere else,' Jim said. 'Does anyone live in the house; besides Gerard, I mean?'

'No, no one. I'm sure of that. He kept telling me how lonely he was, rattling around in that big house all alone. Go get it, Jim,' Linda said with intensity. 'You can do it, and you know what that money means to us.'

'Just tell me how to get there,' Jim Early said, getting to his feet again.

Frank Gerard's house wasn't hard to find. It sat in a pretty little oak-studded valley. With white columns and a well-tended flower garden it seemed terribly out of place in this semi-desert area. Built on ambition, the house itself represented what Gerard had wished to accomplish in Zanzibar. It was built to impress people; it was meant to establish Gerard as Zanzibar's first citizen, to hold dinners and balls, to showcase its successful owner. Most of the materials would have had to be freighted in at great expense. It was no wonder that Gerard was feeling financial cramps, that he craved the Red Bird Saloon, Colin Pippen's less impressive but more authentic temple to wealth.

It was no surprise that Gerard needed to keep Jim Early's money. When the swindle had failed he had gone directly to plain theft. And then to murder. Well, a man of pride and ambition can overextend himself as easily as the poor and humble. Gerard had tried to amass all that he could in Zanzibar, but he had spent too freely. Now among other things he meant to have Linda Lu and Jim's poker winnings.

Those, he could not have.

Jim started his horse down the slope toward the big white house. He gave little thought to what Judge O'Connell would say concerning his tactics. In Jim's mind it was legal to recover what was his, and if the man who was a known swindler and a murderer got in the way, justice, if not the law, deemed that Gerard be dealt with harshly.

Jim Early saw no saddled horses near the house, nor any movement. Could it be that Gerard had gone off and simply left the money where Linda had seen it? Perhaps. Gerard was convinced that he had charmed Linda; he also had his hired gun, Kyle Colson, to worry about. If Gerard had not returned to the cabin to pay Colson, he'd think the gunfighter would return, seeking his blood wages.

Gerard would take steps to prevent that. If he was on the trail to Bedel Road, he might or might not have passed the Pierce brothers' wagon carrying the fallen

144

gunman to Zanzibar.

That might either please the man or panic him. He might conclude that he had underestimated Jim Early.

Jim rode his gray horse directly toward the house, passing through the slender shade cast by the cotton-wood trees. He knew that riding directly to the front of the house was risky but as far as he could tell no one was at home. If there were a rifleman concealed somewhere he would have spotted Jim long ago and could have picked him off easily in that open country, so he felt fairly secure in approaching the house. Besides, what else was there to do?

He had promised Linda that he would recover her money – why not call it that? Somehow Jim's desire to locate the stolen table stakes had faded over the past few days – but he would do his best to keep his promise.

All was silence as Jim swung down from the saddle and hitched his pony to the rail. He stopped and listened before stepping up on to the porch of the white house, but besides the whisper of the light breeze through the cottonwood trees, there was not a sound. Jim stepped up and went to the front door. There, he hesitated a minute.

Jim shouldered the heavy door and it popped open with surprising ease. He eased into the carpeted hallway and met his man. A heavy object, perhaps a fireplace poker, arced toward his head. Jim caught only the shadows of the descending club, but it was enough for him to move his head fractionally and so the iron tore his ear and landed painfully on his shoulder instead of crushing his skull. With his right arm numbed, Jim turned and stepped away from his attacker, who had been hiding behind the door.

'I knew it,' a wide-eyed Frank Gerard said. 'I knew you'd be on your way out here.' The man with the flowing red mustache raised his weapon again, intent on bashing Jim's head in. It was too late; he had had his chance.

Jim stepped immediately forward, his chest colliding with Gerard's. He swung his left fist and it landed solidly on Gerard's jaw. Gerard's left hand lost its hold on the iron and Jim grabbed for his right hand, bending it back on itself until the poker dropped free.

Then, slamming Gerard up against the wall so that a hanging picture fell free and banged against the floor, he began methodically pounding Gerard's body. Gerard fought back, but he was a townsman, smaller, and not as strong as Jim, who drove his fists into Gerard's ribs, belly, and face with vengeful fury.

Jim was struck on the face, on the neck, but he felt little of it. His determination was fixed on putting Gerard down, on finishing the man, and he continued to rain rights and lefts on the overwhelmed man, who now could only try to throw up his arms in futile defense of his face.

Jim drove his left into Gerard's unprotected ribs twice more and then threw a looping overhand right, which caught Gerard on the temple and caused his knees to buckle. The man's eyes went blank and he slid slowly down the wall to sit against the floor, his head cocked to one side, his breathing ragged, blood streaming from his nose. He was out cold.

Jim staggered to the next room where deep-purple drapes hung across wide, arched windows. There were heavy silken ropes of gold with tassels on their ends used to tie the drapes back. Jim yanked hard on one of them and it came free in his hands. Returning to the entranceway he crouched and bound Gerard's hands and feet with the elegant sash. Jim stood over the man, staring down at him. Gerard's clothing was disheveled and torn, his red mustache, normally groomed perfectly, splayed out in all directions. One of his eyes was black and his nose was swollen. Jim took no pleasure in viewing the battered man, only relief that he would not have to tangle with Frank Gerard again on more deadly terms.

Jim started toward the back bedroom Linda had described. His ear was trickling blood and his shoulder was growing stiff. The door to the room, painted in white with gilt trim along the moldings, stood open. There was the fancy white bed where the green bag should be hidden.

Unless Gerard, not so confident after Linda Lu's visit, had taken it and hidden it away on some shelf or cupboard in the large house, which would take hours to search. But overconfidence was one of Gerard's constant traits and, lifting up the skirt of the bedspread, Jim spotted the green bag with its wooden handles and bent to recover it.

Would it be empty? Jim could only hope not. He opened the bag on the bed; inside was the twenty thousand dollars. His money, Linda's money.

It was done. He no longer had to remain the marshal

of Zanzibar, to stay in this dying, slovenly little town, nor concern himself with its tawdry problems. All roads now lay open to him.

Gerard was struggling mightily with his bonds before Jim returned carrying the bag, which lit up Gerard's eyes with anger.

'Why, you. . . !' Gerard began, through painfully swollen lips.

'If you don't want to be gagged, just shut up, Gerard. You're nothing but a thieving pirate yourself.'

It was late in the afternoon, with a red blush staining the western skies, when Jim Early trailed into Zanzibar, Frank Gerard being led behind him on one of his own half-dozen horses. Still tied in golden bonds, Gerard looked foolish enough that taunting men began shouting at the humiliated landowner minutes after they had passed the city limits.

The office was locked and Jim didn't have his key. 'Open up, Tibbs!' he shouted as loudly as he could, knowing that Bernie could be passed out inside. When he heard boots shuffling toward the door he returned to the horse Gerard had been mounted on and tilted him to one side until he slumped into Jim's arms and was planted on his feet. Blinking in confusion, Bernie stood in the open doorway, his shirt only half tucked in, his eyes watery and red.

'Open the cell door, Bernie.'

'Another one?' Tibbs asked. 'When you set out to clean up a town, Jim, I guess you mean to do it.'

As the key was fitted into the lock, Arvin Hinton sat

up and asked, 'Are you finally going to let me out?'

'I just brought you some company, Arvin. You two will be together for a long time. Maybe down in state prison, or possibly you'll visit a gallows together.'

Arvin's cursing was the more vigorous, Frank Gerard's countenance the more dismal as Jim shoved the new man into the cramped little cell.

'There's barely room for one man in here,' Gerard complained as Jim shut the door and locked it.

Through the bars in the cell window, Jim answered, 'Maybe you should bring that up at the next council meeting. Tell them we need a new, larger jail.'

Then Gerard's volume in cursing rose to match the furious Arvin Hinton's.

'Don't bring no one else in for a while, will you, Marshal?' Bernie pleaded. 'These boys aren't going to let a man get any peace around here.'

'They'll shut up after a while. They're bound to run out of words.'

'I suppose,' Bernie replied, 'seeing as they only seem to know about six or seven of them. Meantime,' the deputy said, reaching for his bottle of whiskey, 'I guess there's not much else to do but have a drink. Want to join me, Marshal?'

'No, I guess not. I've still got things to do today, if you think you'll be all right.'

'Oh, I'll be all right,' Bernie said, sitting again. 'Unless they can gnaw their way through four inches of oak wood. If they do,' he said, indicating the pistol on the desk, 'I've got this and they've none.'

'All right. Listen,' Jim said, 'don't let anyone in, and

149

I mean anyone. Not the mayor, not even Judge O'Connell. I haven't had a chance to talk to them yet. I'll tell them why I'm holding Gerard and tell them what evidence I have later.'

'And you have some?'

'I do now – enough to hang Gerard. I wasn't kidding when I said they might both swing for what they've done.'

It had been another long day to tell Linda about, Jim considered as he rode home. But of more importance to her than his little saga would be the green carpetbag riding on the pommel of his saddle. That was all right – he had never asked or expected Linda Lu Finch to be more than she was. Swinging down from the gray's back, Jim went into the house to find Linda wearing a shiny green dress. Her eyes were wide, excited, as they settled on the green bag in his hand.

'I knew you could do it, Jim!' she said. 'Did you have to kill him?'

'No, I threw him in jail.'

After a brief tug of war with the bag, Jim let her have it and sat down. She opened the bag eagerly and smiled, holding up a sheaf of money. 'We have it back! It's all done, thank heavens!' Belatedly she added, 'You look like hell, Jim. Your ear is swollen and bleeding.'

Jim only nodded, half-closing his eyes. His shoulder was roaring with pain. Linda, sitting on the floor, began counting the money. He did not hold her concentration against her – she was only Linda Lu.

'I'll start dividing it up,' she told him. 'Unless you

want to do it while I watch.'

Jim answered, 'I don't really see the point in dividing it.'

'You don't?' Linda asked with some surprise. 'I thought this was the end of the line for us. Being together, I mean.' Jim must have shown his astonishment, because Linda put her hand on his leg and said with gravity in those dark, intent eyes of hers, 'Things have changed so much, Jim.'

'You no longer care for me.'

She sighed. 'Of course I do, that's why I want what's best for you – for both of us.'

'I'm afraid I don't understand,' Jim said.

'Yes you do, Jim. You just don't want to admit it,' Linda said in a calm voice. 'I can't stay here in this ragged little town, you know that. But you! Jim, I believe you have carved out a home for yourself in Zanzibar, and I believe that you like it. You are respected here. You have a little jail that you built yourself. The towns-people trust you.

'Jim, I will never feel comfortable here, but I think you do. I am a city girl, as you well know, whereas you are a country man. What would you do without a horse and a gun? You can't want to just sit by and watch me be frivolous, throwing my money away – and I will.

'This town needs you, Jim ... and I think you need it.'

'I think . . .' Jim began.

'And there's a little blonde girl who wants you as well. She'd be a much better wife for you than I would, Jim. You know that.'

'I don't even know her!' Jim objected. 'Not really.'

'I think you do. I think that's just one more thing you don't want to admit.' She scooted nearer. 'Jim, I don't want to be only a habit, a convenience to you. You deserve better and so do I.'

'But what will you do?'

'Pack my clothes and hire a man to take me and my trunk to the nearest stage stop. Then I'm off for Santa Fe, Jim. And I won't be one bit sorry about any of it, things we did. Nor should you feel that way, Jim Early – get back on your horse and ride into Zanzibar; take that young girl out to dinner. She's probably never been invited out in this town, not with the kind of men they have around here.'

'But—'

'And change your shirt first, there's blood all over it.'

TWELVE

Jim Early rode silently back through the settling purple dusk. He felt rejected, relieved, encouraged, and optimistic all at once. He had protested a little more, but Linda was convinced that she was right, and in the end he was forced to see that she probably was. He had work to do in the morning, people to talk to. Mayor Hazlitt, Peter Wiley, and Judge O'Connell would want to be informed about all of the recent events, especially where they concerned Frank Gerard. And he had plenty to tell them. Then there was the business of talking to Colin Pippen again, either alone or in concert with the council members and Judge O'Connell. Jim remained convinced that a compromise could be worked out between the saloon-keeper and the town.

After that he would have to sit down with the judge and come to an agreement about what laws would be enforced. Jim found he favored an ordinance forbidding the discharge of firearms in the city limits, but not forbidding men from actually carrying their guns – that would prove troublesome and probably impossible to enforce.

From there Jim meant to move on to the building of a new, larger jail; if he was going to arrest men, he had to have a place to keep them. Then, too, he would need a steady, sober deputy until Warren Dodge was fit enough to return – assuming Warren wanted to give it another try after being shot his first day on the job.

What else? Oh, yes, he would have to find a new place to live. Staying in Gerard's cottage was not an option – besides, there were liable to be legal entanglements with all of the man's property. Well, Jim thought with a shrug, he could afford it now. He possessed something under ten thousand dollars, had a job and an acquaintance with the leading men of Zanzibar, an incomplete, but mostly amiable knowledge of and relationship with its inhabitants.

He had hopes of a new love, although he did not know how deeply Ginnie's feelings ran toward him, but he would move slowly and find out soon enough. And, she did own a small ranch. He wondered . . . Jim had to rein his thoughts in; they were running far ahead of him.

All right, then, he thought as he reached the town limits again, he would begin with a dinner at the Strawberry Heights Hotel tonight if Ginnie was willing to go out with him. He knew that she was a waitress all day long, but that didn't mean she didn't get hungry herself. And new, brighter surroundings might be just what she needed. Jim would tell her about Gerard and how she no longer had a reason to fear the conniving skunk. Then let the conversation ramble where it would.

He would miss Linda Lu, he truly would, but he had known of her longing for a big town when he had first rescued her. It was Linda who had suggested taking Ginnie out to dinner, and he thought she probably knew what she was talking about. The longer he knew Linda, the more he had come to realize how often she was right.

He also knew that spending much longer in Zanzibar would drive a wedge of discontent between them. She had made his decision easy for him. He could only promise to think of her now and then and hope she could spare the time to do the same for him.

Jim swung from the gray horse in the alley beside Ethel M's, thinking he might find Ginnie out back. It would be easier to talk to her there than inside a busy restaurant. But the back door to the restaurant was closed and she was not around. Jim stepped down to tie his horse to the hitch rail there.

'I figured you'd show up here sooner or later, Early,' the somehow-familiar voice said from out of the shadows.

'Billy?' Jim asked, turning toward the sound of the voice.

'It's me, Jim. We're going over to bust my brother out of jail.'

'It won't do any good, Billy. Arvin can't ride.'

'You saw to that, didn't you?'

Jim could not see the black-bearded convict in the darkness. Jim, himself, made a fine target in his fresh white shirt, the light spilling out from the restaurant window behind him.

'You fixed him up fine, blowing Arvin's ankle apart.'

'He drew down on me, Billy. What was I to do, stand there and take it?'

'Let's get moving,' Billy said in a taut voice. Jim could still not see Billy Hinton well in this poor light, but he saw the man make a move toward him. He would obviously have his pistol in hand. 'We're popping Arvin out of that cracker box. Walk this way. We're going around the back way.'

'No,' Jim said, standing firm. 'I can't do that, Billy.'

'Because you're wearing a badge now, or because you're not very smart? I'll kill you, Early, I swear I will.'

'They'd hang you for that – in this town.'

'If they caught me,' Billy said. He still had not come forward out of the shadows. 'It'd be almost worth it to know I'd gotten even with you for your treachery.'

'Are you still thinking about the Clovis bank job?' Jim asked. 'If you two had spent as much time thinking about it as you have sulking about it, you'd realize that I couldn't possibly have had anything to do with the missing money in that bank.'

'I know, and you just left before the law came because you felt sorry for some old farm couple and didn't want to take their money!' Billy's voice was heavy with sarcasm, drenched with hatred.

'I'm not the one who bought you a prison term, nor Arvin's new troubles,' Jim said. 'If you and Arvin just left me alone here—'

'Alone with all your money and fancy women? To

hell with you, Jim Early! Are you going to walk over to the jail with me or not?'

'No, Billy. No, I'm not.'

The outer door to the kitchen of Ethel M's swung open and a shaft of light was sprayed into the alley, plainly illuminating the figure of Billy Hinton. Billy threw up one hand to shield his eyes, the other, holding his blue Colt revolver, swung up toward Jim Early.

Jim drew, fired wildly and flung himself to one side as Billy's pistol thundered in the confines of the alley and a bullet whipped past Jim's head to thud into the siding of the restaurant.

Billy was down and writhing in pain, holding his knee. Jim found himself unhurt. Ginnie Cummings was standing on the loading dock screaming. She rushed down into the alley and toward Jim as the marshal walked to Billy, kicked his gun aside, and cautiously bent over the flailing, kicking, cursing ex-con. A few men had gathered at the head of the alley, watching.

Ginnie flung herself into Jim's arms and held on tightly. Her tears streaked her face and his. 'You're all right,' she said over and over. Finally, Jim held her at arm's length and said:

'Yes, I am. Want to go out to dinner tonight?' Still stunned, she could not answer the unexpected question just then, and so he decided to leave it till later. One of the other waitresses had come out to hurry Ginnie away from the scene. Jim turned and motioned to a couple of bystanders.

To Billy Hinton, he said, 'Come on, Billy. Now I'll take you to see your brother.'

'Well, I guess your aim's improving a little,' a whiskey-soaked Bernie Tibbs said from behind the desk in the marshal's office as Ben Lovesy worked over the wounded Billy Hinton. Arvin was at the cell window, gripping the bars as he watched. Billy's trousers had been cut away and Lovesy was doing the best he could for Billy's shattered knee.

'I mean,' Bernie said in a slurred voice, 'the other one you got in the ankle, this one in the knee. Maybe you'll bring your aim up a little and get the next one in the crotch, and eventually get where you want to be.'

'I know what you meant,' Jim said with a sourness that could not disguise his pleasure in having taken Billy Hinton down – without getting shot himself.

'It's a wonder you ever got that Kyle Colson, Marshal,' Bernie persisted.

'I drowned him,' Jim reminded the deputy.

'Oh, that's right. Well,' Bernie said, reaching for his ever-present bottle, 'maybe you ain't the slickest I ever seen, but you are efficient, I've got to give you that.'

Jim found he did not care a bit about the wounded man's suffering, but thought it was right to ask, 'How is he, Lovesy?'

The little white-haired man moved away from his patient. 'You have to ask me? You're the one who drilled him through the knee. It's torn up real bad, Marshal. Bones like a bag full of marbles. He'll probably pull through, but he sure won't ever walk right again. He'd be better off if I just took the leg off and

158

fitted him for a peg leg.'

'I knew it!' Arvin Hinton shouted from his cell. 'The man's a maniac, Early! All he can think of doing is sawing men's necessaries off.'

'Neither of them's ever going to ride again, that's for certain,' Bernie Tibbs drawled. 'It's a good enough way to break up a gang of thieves, I suppose.'

'I suppose,' Jim said. He was suddenly weary now that the excitement in his blood had eased. 'So's returning them to prison, which is probably where they're bound. Do you need anything, Bernie?'

'You're going out again?' Bernie asked, perplexed.

'Yes, I am. I have a pretty lady and a fancy dinner waiting for me.'

'Some men have all the luck,' Bernie Tibbs said.

'Don't they?' Jim Early answered.